MORE BOOKS BY
DAISY PRESCOTT

Love with Altitude:
Next to You
Crazy Over You
Wild for You (coming later in 2017)
Up to You (2018)

Modern Love Stories:
We Were Here (prequel to Geoducks)
Geoducks Are for Lovers
Wanderlust
Happily Ever Now (coming late 2017)

Wingmen:
Ready to Fall
Confessions of a Reformed Tom Cat
Anything but Love
Small Town Scandal (coming May 2017)

Bewitched
A magical short set in Salem, Massachusetts
Spellbound
A magical sequel to Bewitched
Enchanted
A magical continuation (coming September 2017)

CRAZY OVER YOU

A LOVE WITH ALTITUDE NOVEL

DAISY PRESCOTT

Cover Design by ©SM Lumetta

Images from Stocksy and Depositphotos.com

Editing: There for You Editing

Proofreading: Proofing Style

Interior Design & Formatting: Type A Formatting

For my Colorado family

ONE

MARA

I FORCE MYSELF to inhale a deep, steadying breath.

Closing my eyes, I attempt to picture my happy place.

My mind wanders to the mountains. Majestic, snow-covered jagged peaks.

Bad idea. Instead of relaxing, I begin hyperventilating again.

I need a new happy place.

With my eyes closed, I swear someone or something big is standing on my chest.

I listen for the sounds of heavy breathing from a bear. This would explain my inability to breathe. While I've been stuck lying on a mogul, the icy cold seeping through my ski pants, a bear has stealthily climbed on top of me.

Honestly, I've always imagined bears, especially wild bears, would be smellier.

I can't even be Goldilocks in my own twisted version of the Three Bears. Figures.

With a shudder, I manage to suck enough air into my lungs to expand them, bringing oxygen to my blood and eventually to my brain. Feeling about forty percent less likely to pass out, I open my eyes.

There's no bear.

Only a steep precipice of death stretching below me.

Naming something so horrible after fancy jewelry is a terrible abuse of language. A big, fat lie set up to deceive. Double-black diamond sounds like a pair of lovely stud earrings.

Not a white, icy maw of death.

Foolishly, I stare beyond my boot-bound feet still strapped to my skis. Below me is a snow-covered right angle lined with fearless evergreens. There's nothing sloping about it.

I've survived the part of the run between basalt cliff and certain death. How silly of me to have been lured into false confidence of my survival by a lovely wooden bench perched at the edge of sanity, overlooking the snowcapped beauty of Mt. Daly sparkling in the sunshine like a postcard.

There wouldn't be a charming park bench if this run were a dangerous threat to both life and limb. A place to sit typically implies safety and comfort, places where grandmothers and small children gather. Or old men playing chess.

Although, sometimes lonely people go to parks to contemplate their lives and replay all the bad decisions they've made.

In that case, the bench is perfectly situated.

If this were a movie, I could rewind and keep myself from skiing past the salvation of a bench. I could avoid making yet another rash decision.

Let's keep rewinding the video until I'm packing up a U-haul and saying good-bye to Boston. Kissing my sweet, boring boyfriend, Geoffrey, one final time while ignoring his hints about visiting me in Colorado.

Hell, speed things up and erase him entirely. Eager, average, and missionary-position-sex-followed-by-spooning Geoffrey who nearly passed out when I told him about my first time neutering a cat. Bless him and his love for optometry.

"Eyes are the windows to the soul," he used to say. "So that makes

me a soul doctor."

No, Geoffrey, no, it doesn't.

Is this the part where my life flashes before my eyes?

I need something less depressing to think about.

The sheer drop-off comes to mind.

As do broken limbs, bruised ribs, cracked skull, loss of dignity, and tears, so many tears.

And avalanches. Giant walls of life-crushing snow racing down the mountain. Because death is what happens in the wilds of nature.

It's a long list of awful things.

Straight ahead of me, across a plunging valley, is a lovely view of a rust-colored hill. A thin black road winds along the bottom. The cold wind howls in the canyon and whistles through the bare branches of aspens hugging the hills. On my right is a grove of pine trees and deep snow. I think about scooting over to them, burrowing into the well at the base of a trunk and hibernating until I can walk down the mountain in the spring mud.

Downside is this plan would require movement.

A few skiers fly down the run, catching air at the top behind me and landing in soft clouds of powder before sluicing down the Mountain of Doom in a blur of expensive ski gear.

An image of a frog crossing a five-lane highway pops into my head.

I'm going to spoil it for you: it doesn't end well for the frog. Splat.

"Watch out!" a male voice shouts from above me, which is also behind me.

I think he wants me to move. As if I've wandered into the middle of the slalom course at the Olympics and set up a picnic like I'm Yogi Bear.

I wish I were a happy-go-lucky bear with a stolen picnic

basket. Obviously, I have bears on the brain.

Instead, I'm sitting here having a panic attack on a ski slope. Of this I'm hyper-aware.

I brace for impact. Hoping against all laws of physics whoever collides with me is a handsome, rugged, intellectual, animal lover, who miraculously scoops me into his arms and skis down the rest of the run while simultaneously falling in love with me at first sight.

Sadly, neither happens. Mr. Voice blurs past me without a second glance after his warning.

I eye the tree line and ponder the odds of successfully stopping myself before plunging through the trees and ending up a cautionary tale.

She wasn't wearing a helmet would be the lead.

In a misplaced effort to reclaim a shred of dignity, I awkwardly adjust my bright red and white knit hat with the oversized pom-pom on the top. Not an easy feat while wearing ski gloves.

My snow bunny dreams are shredded and perched atop a heap of other silly fantasies I've had in my life. Like taking Nick Jonas's infamous virginity when I was in high school. Or suddenly being able to ski double-black diamond runs. Or being the kind of girl who has wild one-night stands instead of dating the safe, yet boring Geoffries of the world. None of those things are true.

More skiers crest the top of the run and fly by me in colorful blurs.

Why are there so many skiers with death wishes today? Who are all these people?

Although, it is a beautiful day to die. Inches of powder from last night's storm freshen the snowpack into a glittering white. The sun shines in a cloudless sky the color of sapphires thanks to the lack of oxygen in the high altitude. I'm sure people wheezing for oxygen on Everest think the same thing.

Another bad idea.

Reminding myself of the lowered percentage of oxygen speeds up my breathing again.

My heart thumps faster, creating a *whooshing* sound of blood in my ears.

Is it suddenly hot?

I feel hot.

Could be the blazing sun. That's probably it.

What are the first signs of hypothermia?

Leaning back, I do the one thing my earth science teacher, Mrs. Roe, made me swear I'd never, ever do. I stare at the pale sun. I'm living on the edge, literally. What do I have to lose?

I remind myself I'm sitting in a pile of snow and the temperature probably hovers near thirty.

I wonder if I'll ever see thirty.

More crazy people ski by me while I begin writing my obituary.

Dr. Mara Keiley, DVM, 28, recently of Snowmass Village, Colorado, foolishly believed she was confident and skilled enough to tackle a double-black diamond run after years of being a solid teal skier—a low risk combination of blue and green slopes. She is mourned, and judged for her poor decision making by her parents, Raymond and Sheryl Keiley, who always wanted a doctor in the family, a real, human doctor, not a veterinarian, and her younger brother, Todd, who played high school football, and is still the favorite child. She was unmarried, single, and a size twelve at the time of her death, but not a virgin. Dr. Keiley is survived by two cats and a dog of dubious origin.

Nailed it.

Sounds about right if my mother is put in charge of writing it. Perfectly captures her vague, passive aggressive disappointment. If only she knew, she'd be thrilled my last thoughts are of her.

"Hey," another man shouts from above me, "are you okay? You, in the red hat. Hello?"

His deep, resonant voice and confident delivery remind me of a movie trailer narrator.

Twisting to see behind me, I lean too far to the left, shifting my body weight, and slide downhill sideways. In an attempt to right myself, I lift my left ski pole and stab it into the snow.

Brilliant.

Now I'm lying with my head downhill and my legs spread eagle, skis akimbo. A pole rests a few feet away. Sitting up to reclaim it requires stronger ab muscles than I possess. I should've listened about strengthening my core.

I can't even think "core" without cringing. I blame my grandmother's romance novels I snuck as a kid. *Her core trembled as Sir Reginald stroked her slick folds.* Shudder. A girl can learn many things about the ways of love and throbbing manhoods by sneaky reading romances.

With the sun in my eyes, I can't clearly make out the face of the speaker, but I recognize his red and black uniform. White crosses decorate the chest and sleeve.

He's ski patrol.

Thank you, God.

"Are you injured?" he calls down to me.

"Only my pride," I mumble into my jacket.

"Anything broken?" he continues as if I haven't spoken.

"No, I'm fine." I raise my voice so he can hear me.

"You don't look fine. Think you can right yourself and uphill? Climb back to me?" I can't see his eyes behind his reflective goggles, but I can hear the smile in his voice. I can't tell if it's friendly or condescending.

"I think I'm kind of wedged in here." I use my remaining ski pole to gesture at my skis jutting out of the snow at right angles.

"I can see that. Can you pop yourself out of your bindings?

Use the big, long stick in your hand."

"You use your big stick," I mumble as I jab at my bindings. If shooting fish in a barrel is easy, spearing them must be the opposite.

I fail.

"Never as easy as it looks." He executes a small hop and glides down the mountain like a commercial for men's deodorant. Or beer. Something manly and smooth. Razors.

He's like a damn razor commercial with his smooth moves. His legs barely move as he turns.

A yard or so above me, he plants a black pole and floats to a stop a foot away from my skis. Without another word, he snaps me out of both bindings. One ski has decided it would rather finish the run without me and slides downhill on its own. I can't blame it. Clearly, I'm not the most fun.

Both feet coast downhill in a slow windmill to my left, leaving me parallel to the slope and no longer splayed out like the world's least sexy, down-padded centerfold.

For anyone keeping score at home:

Mara Keiley, one.

Mountain of Doom, five. Or ten.

I've lost count.

My savior scoops up the other ski and hands it to me before retrieving the one trying to pretend it doesn't know me. As he sidesteps his way back up to me, I manage to sit up.

"Here you go." He sets the ski uphill from me. "You think you can make it down?"

Still wearing his goggles, he resembles an astronaut or a spaceman from the future. All I can see of his face is his strong nose and dark scruff that's somewhere between beard and stubble—less than a hipster and more than Ryan Reynolds. From the bump, I'm guessing his nose has probably been broken at least once. I wonder if the break came from fights or sports.

His full lips are an unfair deep rose color. Surprisingly, they're not chapped.

I don't know why I expect them to be chapped. Days spent in the sun on the slopes would probably make me look like I'd been living in the olden days without lip balm or sunscreen. I bet he's an amazing kisser. His lips would feel incredible pressed against mine.

Men are so lucky.

I've always had a thing for beards. Ever since I made out with a random guy on a dare in vet school.

They're my chocolate cake.

I'm unable to resist either.

"Did you hit your head?" His deep, rumbly voice sounds closer.

Twisting my neck, I realize he's crouching next to my side now.

"You should be wearing a helmet. They're not mandatory, but we recommend them. Especially if you're going to tackle the more advanced runs."

I pat the pom-pom on my hat. "I'm fine. I sat down before I fell."

"That was smart." He stands to remove his skis, spikes both pairs into the snow behind us, and then sits next to me. "So you're just taking in the view?"

"I missed the bench and it's a lovely vista." As I swing my arm out, I manage to slap his shoulder. "Sorry."

"No problem." He shoves his goggles to the crown of his own helmet. "I wouldn't advise hanging out on a ski slope."

"Thanks." I stare straight ahead. "I wouldn't recommend having a panic attack on one either." At the words, my heart rate picks up.

"Is that what happened?" Genuine concern changes the timbre of his voice.

"I was okay until the top of this run. I survived the road of certain extinction with rocks on one side and death on the other. Figured I was safe. Then I hit the top of this section and too much adrenaline hit me. I shouldn't be here. I'm not this kind of girl."

His shoulders lift with amusement. "Not what kind of girl?"

The kind of girl who would notice the drop in his voice and how the words come out sounding less like a question and more like hopeful lust. I wonder if women create fake reasons all day long to meet cute ski patrol on the mountain. How far would some women go?

All the way. They'd go all the way.

They'd do whatever it takes to meet a cute guy.

"No, not *that* kind of girl. I should've stayed with the blue runs. I'm comfortable with blue. Blue is a great color. The sky, the ocean. They're both blue. And water. Like snow."

His shoulders shake. "Thanks for the science lesson."

"Stop laughing at me. I could've died."

"Not on my watch. I haven't lost a skier yet. I woke up in a good mood this morning, so I know today's not the day to have that record broken by a beautiful woman who likes to take risks."

My cheeks heat, but I let his compliment slip away without commenting. Is this all part of the snow bunny and skier dance? Or is he distracting me with praise?

It's working.

"I don't suppose there's a way off this side of the mountain that doesn't involve the words black or diamond?"

"Sadly, only one. Do you need the toboggan?"

Oh, hell no.

I duck my chin. I can feel the giant pom-pom on my hat droop forward. "Maybe."

"I have another solution."

"Does it involve further humiliation?"

"No, of course not. I can ski you down to the lift. You'll have to go back up to get to the village, but you'll have your choice of green and blue runs down to Fanny Hill. Or I can call for the toboggan . . ." His words trail off as he grabs the radio strapped to his chest.

Images of him skiing with me in his arms flash through my mind. "You'd carry me?"

He releases a surprised chuckle. "I would if necessary, but I'm thinking you'll ski down with my help."

The picture of him lifting me into his arms as if I weigh nothing and the two of us swooping off into the distance fades.

"How?" I peek at his profile.

"I'll ski and you'll hold onto my pole."

Mara, do not make this dirty.

He shifts to stand and holds out his hand. "Think you can manage that?"

"You want me to trust you with my life?" I eye his glove, but don't reach for it.

"I do. I'm more than qualified." He points a gloved hand to the cross emblem on his sleeve. "See? Want a list of my credentials?"

I remain sitting. "Shouldn't you have a St. Bernard with a barrel of whiskey around its neck to revive me?"

"First of all, my dog's a Norwegian duck tolling retriever mix, and Fern's too young to drink. Second, St. Bernards carry brandy."

"Get a lot of ducks up here needing rescuing?"

"Only chicks." He fights a grin and a dimple of suppression reveals itself on his left cheek. Dimples are the sprinkles on top of chocolate cake, and his reminds me of someone.

I narrow my eyes at his bad, and pretty sexist pun. Since he literally holds my life in his hands, I decide to stick to the safe subject of canines.

"You have a work dog? Like an avalanche dog?" I accept his hand to be lifted up.

"Not like. Is. Hardest working member of ski patrol." He lets go of my hand to position my skis.

"I don't suppose you have a flask in your backpack?" I gesture at the black bag I'm pretty sure is filled with first aid supplies.

He shakes his head. "Not even a thermos of cocoa."

I finally meet his kind eyes. The irises are a surprising light, warm caramel brown with darker brown near the edge. They remind me of crème brûlée. Chocolate cake might be my favorite, but I wouldn't kick a nice crème brûlée out of bed.

His eyes are also vaguely familiar.

"Miss?"

I continue staring. "Yes?"

"Where are you from?"

"Here."

When he frowns, I notice he has a scar over his left eyebrow and a little divot on his right cheekbone. From chicken pox? The dimple on his cheek doesn't show unless he's grinning or fighting a smile. There's a mix of blond and red in his dark scruff. I wonder what his hair looks like not stuck under a helmet.

His voice interrupts my cataloging of his features. "You mean you're visiting? Or you live here? I'd remember you if you were a local."

"I live in Snowmass. Just moved here two weeks ago, right after New Year's."

He purses his lips and remains silent. His dimple makes another appearance as he stops himself from speaking.

"You?" I ask, trying to keep the conversation flowing to distract myself.

"I live here. Ski patrol, remember?"

"Oh, right. Of course." I'm nailing the small talk.

"Not that I can afford a place in Aspen. Or Snowmass. Fern and I live near Woody Creek."

Unless he has a dog and a wife with the same name, he's not married. I file this information away, along with his dimple and scars.

"Ready? You need to put your skis back on now so we can get you down the mountain."

"Oh, right." My focus shifts to my feet. Somewhat gracefully, I manage to click into my bindings and not fall on my ass or slide down the mountain on my butt. Apparently, my panic attack erased all but the basic skiing abilities.

"Great job." He uses a voice probably reserved for his wonder dog and small children. Once I'm upright and steady, he uses his radio to call someone. "Ski patrol, Jesse. I have a ten-fourteen. Female, late twenties. No injuries. Escorting to Campground chairlift."

"Ten-four," a female voice responds.

"Is ten-fourteen special code for girl freak out?" I brush off the snow on my butt.

"Non-injury escort." He's all business again as he clicks into his bindings and adjusts his pack.

"Let's get this over with." Forcing optimism into my voice, I straighten my back.

He sidesteps in front of me and positions himself to my left, extending a ski pole in my direction. "Grab my pole."

I press my lips together to hold back an embarrassing snicker. Unfortunately, ducking my head allows me to sneak a peek at his crotch. Not that I can see anything.

Stupid baggy ski pants.

"Here we go. Keep your hands and feet inside the ride at all times," he announces like he's the ride manager of the Matterhorn at Disneyland. He shifts his body weight and we slide downhill.

Even though we're moving slowly, I close my eyes when I feel my chest constrict.

"You might feel better with your eyes open." His voice is calm and confident.

With a shake of my head, I tell him my opinion of this suggestion.

"Suit yourself."

The wind against my cold cheek warns me he's picked up speed. In response, I lock my knees and tighten my grip.

"Uh, uh, uh. Eyes open. Bend your knees. Loosey goosey, please."

In spite of my fear of dying, I laugh. Laughing makes me open my eyes. "Did you just say—"

"Loosey goosey? Yes. I can give you a ski school pep talk, if that'll help."

"Still using pizza slices and french fries? That's how I learned."

"It's the universal language of beginning skiers." He gives me a warm smile over his shoulder. "You doing okay?"

"Can we rest for a minute?" My heart is racing, but I'm not sure if it's from him or the cliff we're sliding down.

He makes a turn and slows to a stop on a large bump. "You okay?"

"Mmm hmm." My nod turns into a shake. Blood rushes in my ears as I take calming breaths. "Not really. Keep talking."

"What brings you to Snowmass?" He glances behind him to check our position on the slope.

"I'm the new vet for Hawks Creek Ranch. Elizabeth Hawks and Sage Blum run it." I blow out an exhale to the count of ten.

"The animal rescue and sanctuary?"

"The very one." I smile because I'm thrilled to have my dream job.

He smiles back. "I know Sage. She's with a friend of mine."

"You know Lee?" Where Sage is petite and ethereal, her boyfriend, Lee, is a South African rugby player with movie star good looks.

"We've played rugby together. He takes it a lot more seriously than I do. He could've played pro."

"Not you?" Jesse is tall and broad enough to play a full contact sport.

Not touching the idea of full contact with him with a ski pole.

Nope.

I sigh as I think of full naked contact. I'm in a bit of a dry spell since deciding to break it off with Geoffrey before the holidays.

"I've never been competitive enough. I started playing a couple of years ago for fun. Turns out my aggression makes me good in a scrum."

I have a vague idea about scrums, but nod like I understand the correlation. "You don't seem like an asshole."

"I'm paid to be a nice guy." He gives me a sweet smile while his eyes shine with mischief.

"You're only nice when you're being paid?" I squint at him with distrust.

"You make me sound like a male escort." His smile falters, but the mischievous spark in his warm eyes doesn't fade.

"Your words not mine."

"Better than a stripper. At least I don't have to prance around on stage in a thong." He chuckles.

But I'm not laughing.

Stripper.

The word echoes around in my head as a strong sense of déjà vu hits me smack in the face.

Me dancing on a bar in a short, silver dress. Me practically showing off the goods to a crowd of cheering men.

Oh no. Oh shit.

No. No. NO.

Friends, we have a problem.

My savior isn't prince charming.

No, I'm not that lucky.

He's my worst nightmare.

He's my one-night stand from two years ago.

And he doesn't remember me.

TWO

Two Years Ago

MARA

SEE THE GIRL up there, shaking her ass and bending over to flash her cleavage at the crowd of clapping people below her?

The one who happily did a blow job shot off the bar without using her hands a few minutes before the dancing began?

The girl who can't stop laughing?

She's having the best vacation of her life.

That's me.

I'm the girl on the bar.

When my foot slips on a wet spot and I lose my balance, I don't fall into a heap on the floor. Oh no. I swan dive into the crowd where big manly hands catch me in the best re-creation of the big move in *Dirty Dancing*.

Where's the video of this moment to show the future grandkids?

See how Super Girl—that's me—shows her gratitude with a sloppy kiss right then and there? Full tongue action in the middle of the bar while people whoop?

Yes, actual whooping, my friends.

And I don't even know his name.

Nor do I care.

Tall, dark, and handsome slides me down the front of his body and gently places me back on solid ground. He kindly holds my ass to keep me balanced while making me dizzy with his kiss.

It's possible the dizziness is from the booze fest of the evening catching up with me.

I'd rather pretend he's my perfect kissing match.

Yes, some people are terrible kissers, but most of us manage to get it right. It all comes down to a matter of preference. Maybe there's someone out there who loves open mouth tongue kisses as much as you do. Or is also a fan of the nibbles. Nibblers unite! I'm sure the girl with dry mouth appreciates a man who gives sloppy, wet kisses.

It's all a matter of finding a kissing match.

Mystery man is mine.

I have plans for him.

Big plans if the size of his hands mean anything.

Please let the old adage be true.

Please let big hands mean big other things.

And not feet.

I mean his penis.

Thank you.

The need for oxygen forces me to break away from his amazing kissing lips as I try to catch my breath.

Everything overwhelms my senses. Stuffy air clogs my lungs. Lights pulse and swirl around me. Music blares. The bass thumps so loud it resonates deep inside my ribcage.

At least I think it's the bass. It could be my heart. An after effect of his kiss.

"I need some fresh air." Turning away, I stumble toward the door.

I attempt to navigate the crowd, but no one will move out

of my way. Mystery kisser steps in front of me and leads the way with his big hands and his tall height.

He's the human version of one of those ice breaker ships in the Antarctic. I am a tiny, happy penguin swimming in his wake.

The push of people near the front door blocks our exit. There's no way this crowd isn't breaking fire codes and capacity laws.

"Too many people," I shout. "There's no escape."

A big guy shoulders me and I lose my grip on his hand. The crowd begins to swallow me like a zombie horde. I try to protest, but shouts about Jell-O shots drown out my voice.

This is the story of my life.

I'm shoved and pushed back in the direction I came from. With the determination of a horny salmon, I force myself against the current. I need fresh air soon or someone's going to get their shoes ruined.

It's hopeless. I'm about to give up when strong arms wrap around me and suddenly I'm airborne.

"Come on, Tony, let's get out of here."

"Did you call me Tony?" I don't really have a choice but to go with him, considering I'm currently resting over his shoulder like a fifty-pound bag of dog food.

More like a hundred and fifty pounds.

Okay, one sixty.

Doesn't matter because the way he carries me is effortless.

The chaos calms once we step outside the bar. The chill of the air cools the sweat on my skin. Inhaling, I suck in as much oxygen as the high altitude will allow.

He sets me on my feet.

"Better?" His voice is deep and rumbly near my ear.

Focused on breathing, I nod. I force a lungful of air and slowly count while exhaling. Then I repeat the steps twice more to assure myself I'm not going to hurl.

"You put on quite the show back there. You a professional dancer?"

I sputter. "Like a stripper?"

The tips of his ears go red. "You say it like it's a bad thing?"

I'm about to launch into a diatribe about years spent in labs and a pile of student loan debt, but instead, I remain silent.

"Okay, I'm guessing you're not a stripper and don't take it as a compliment."

I'm stunned silent.

"It's a compliment. You've got moves."

"Like a stripper?" I double-check to make sure I'm not standing here with my boobs hanging out of my silver dress.

All clear. Nothing's exposed. No nip slippage or public panty party.

Tall, dark, and big chuckles. "It was meant to be flattering. I swear."

He's probably used to women throwing themselves at him or curling around his massive frame like a sloth in its favorite tree.

I'm closer to a sloth than I am a stripper. Give me a cozy pair of fuzzy pajamas or a onesie instead of a thong and deathtrap platform heels any night of the week. If I had to choose a vice, it would be sloth. Not lust.

Unless the lusting is after cake.

Or Ryan Reynolds.

Or Ryan Reynolds with cake.

I wipe the side of my mouth to check for drool.

Come on, who wouldn't be drooling over that combination?

Plus, he has such a dirty, dirty mouth in *Deadpool*.

I wonder if Big Hands talks dirty.

He's speaking again, but I'm barely paying attention. When he stops, I glance down to see he's extending his hand. Like a gentleman. Or a guy who's about to tell me how nice it was to meet me, but sadly he has to go home to feed his Sea Monkeys or sort his recycling.

Both have happened to me before.

Look for my autobiography, *True Stories from the Dating Life of Mara Keiley,* on the Cautionary Tales shelf of in the Self Help section in your local bookstore. Or in true life horror stories.

In case you didn't know, Sea Monkeys aren't even remotely monkeys. It's all a huge lie promoted by the brine shrimp conglomeration. Some guy named Harold "invented" them in the fifties. He's probably cousins or best friends with the Pet Rock "inventor," and whoever came up with Chia Pets.

I'm going to state right here, right now: shrimp, rocks, and sprouts are *not* pets.

Not even remotely.

I speak from experience. My parents bought me all three of these so-called pets during my childhood whenever I begged them for a dog, a cat, or the compromise pets, hamsters and guinea pigs.

I never asked for a horse. Or even a pony.

All I wanted was a small dog, but not too small. One who wouldn't shed or bark or bite. Maybe a terrier with manners. A low-key poodle. Or a corgi with an under-active thyroid.

I got a keychain pet.

Later I found out my brother was allergic to fur.

Ironic given he had a hairy back. In high school.

I bet tall, dark, and big doesn't have a hairy back.

I've been cataloguing fake pets while he's standing in front of me, staring at me with a slight smile playing at the corner of his mouth. His lips are so pretty. For a guy. I bet he uses lip balm.

I want to confirm this hypothesis by pressing my lips against his again.

Instead, I'm standing here gawking at him like a fish.

Fish also make terrible pets.

"Sorry. What?" Clearly, my flirting game is so lit it's on fire.

"Asked if you were okay." The playful smile spreads into a grin. "Thought I lost you there for a while."

"I think I might be drunk." A giggle erupts at the end of my sentence, causing me to sway. I'm super unsteady on my feet. Clutching his T-shirt for balance, I attempt to stop being a weirdo. "Sorry."

"For being drunk or petting my chest?"

So much for playing it cool. I focus on my hands, which of their own volition, are pressed against his pecs through the thin cotton of his shirt.

Pressing. Petting. Let's not get caught up in semantics.

I pull my hands away from his chest, but he stops me.

"I didn't say I didn't like it."

Oh.

Okay then. I spread out my fingers and touch as much of his broad man chest as possible.

"This is nice."

His laughter vibrates and rumbles beneath my fingertips.

He's laughing at me again.

I'm clearly tipsy.

Which makes me yet another drunk vacation girl. I'm a cliché.

Delightful.

Sofie will be proud of me. She's the one who dared me to get up on the bar. I think she was leading the shouting to kiss him.

Wait. Where's Sofie?

Last I saw she was helping me up on the bar and cheering.

I look around. Right. She's probably still inside.

"I should go find my friend," I mumble to his pecs as responsibility sobers me.

"Tall with dark hair?" He lifts my chin with a single finger.

"Amazonian tall." I raise my arm above my head to demonstrate. "Often mistaken for the spawn of a supermodel and a giraffe?"

"I think she was the one yelling as I carried you outside."

"What was she saying? Something about protecting my virtue? Begging you to not kidnap her best friend?"

His chest shakes with laughter. "Not exactly. I think she told me to not bring you back until morning and you have condoms in your purse."

Sounds like Sofie. "I have terrible taste in friends."

"Or you have the best kind of friends."

"She's a pusher." Before I launch into a confession of why I need to be pushed, I decide my mouth can be put to better use. I stand on my toes to lessen the height differential between us. The top of my head comes to the top of his biceps.

His eyes focus on my mouth for a brief second before he catches on.

Yep, he definitely has the softest lips ever. The kiss is a study in contrasts. Masculine beard scrapes my skin while the velvet of his lips caresses mine. Heat from his tongue invades my mouth. Sharp teeth nip at the soft flesh of my bottom lip.

He's the best kisser I've ever met.

He really is my kissing soul mate.

I moan, loudly, as I anchor my hands in his messy brown curls. Good luck trying to escape, mister.

He must not mind, because his own hands find a new home on my ass. A not so gentle squeeze pulls me closer, putting me in contact with his groin area. Okay, that's not a sexy word, but better than crotch. Let's move on and focus on the fact he's hard beneath his jeans.

Thanks be to God for proportion.

Without thought, my body begins to rub against him. I'm a cat; he's the scratching post, and boy does this pussy have an itch he can take care of.

I crack myself up and giggle into his mouth.

Which is a terrible thing because he stops kissing me again.

"What so funny?" When he speaks, I feel his warm breath on my cheek.

"Nothing." I press myself against him, trying to remind him how much better making out is than talking.

He narrows his eyes.

I can't tell him. I'll seem like a weird cat lady.

Which I am. Or want to be.

Who dreams of growing up to be a crazy cat lady?

I don't want a hundred cats.

Or a dozen.

I'm studying to be a veterinarian.

To save cats.

And dogs.

Because sea monkeys and fish are not pets.

"It's too ridiculous. If I tell you, you'll think I'm a pervert."

"You were petting my pecs. I already think you're a pervert." His eyes crinkle with amusement. "Plus, you're making out with me and you don't even know my name."

His name never crossed my mind.

"You don't know mine either."

He chuckles. "I tried to introduce myself and you stared at me like I'm a cheeseburger and you're starving."

"Mmm, sounds good."

"Now you really are imagining me as food, aren't you?"

"No, of course not." I stick out my hand. "I'm Mara."

"Jesse." He squeezes my hand. "Don't say it."

"I can't say your name out loud? Are you like He Who Shall Not Be Named?"

"I just told you my name."

"Then you told me not to say it." He's lost me again. I know

I'm still tipsy but he's not making any sense.

With a shake of his head, he tucks me under his arm. I fit perfectly beneath his armpit and I'm grateful he's a believer in deodorant. His warm, pheromone-laden scent envelops me. I may rub my nose along his bicep, inhaling him like a bouquet of roses. Which I hate. Roses. Not a delicious smelling man. I don't want a man to be typical. Geoffrey brings me a single rose wrapped in cellophane I know he buys at the gas station or CVS.

Poor, sweet Geoffrey. He's asked me out three times and I keep saying no.

Shouldn't there be a strikes rule for propositioning someone?

I'd like Jesse to proposition me.

"You feeling okay enough to go back inside?"

I twist around to face the door and the crowd currently screaming for another girl dancing on the bar. "Not really."

"Want me to go find your friend for you?"

"She's a big girl." I laugh at my own pun. "Let's go somewhere else."

Your place.

My condo.

"Only things open now are clubs and bars."

"What about your place?"

"I live down valley. It's kind of a trek for a drink."

"Okay."

"What are you agreeing to?"

I'm not really sure. "How does this normally work?"

"Huh?"

"You pick up a woman and then what?"

He stares at me blankly.

"Are you asking for a timeline?"

"I'm not naïve."

"First, you're the one who jumped into my arms and started kissing me."

"True."

"Second, why do you think I do this on a regular basis?"

My snort is neither ladylike nor quiet.

"You don't even know me." A thin slice of defensiveness coats his words. Either the dude doth protest too much or I've hit a sore spot with my snort.

"I'm sorry. I made assumptions based on your tongue in my mouth and your hands on my ass within minutes of meeting."

"Again, most of that was you. I could be an innocent man who found himself in the wrong place."

A dimple in his left cheek pops out when he tries not to smile.

"Or a lucky guy who was in the right place at the right time," he says as his grin breaks free.

I want to sleep with him.

I'm beyond horny and all this talk, no action, is ruining my buzz . . . and my courage.

Picking up a guy for sex is new for me, but when in Aspen . . .

"We could go back to my condo." I point at the crowd inside the bar. "We'll have it to ourselves. At least until the bars close."

He gives me a lazy smile and lets his eyes sweep over me from hair to heels.

"Okay. Someone should make sure you get home safely."

"Or we could go dancing." If he's only going to escort me to condo, I need more time to convince him I'm irresistible.

"I don't really dance."

"That's nonsense. Everyone can dance."

"I didn't say can't. I said don't. There's a big difference."

I scrunch up my face and boink him on the nose. "Quit with your double-speak and let's go."

Softly, so I barely hear him, he mumbles, "Looks like someone got her second wind."

"One hundred percent. I have amazing rebound skills."

I leave the double-meaning hanging between us.

"Is that what this is all about? Are you on the rebound? Some guy back home break your heart?"

"Last year's news."

"So you're single?"

"As the old Beyoncé song." I hold up my left hand and wiggle my bare fingers. "Come on, let's have some fun."

He opens his mouth and I assume he's going to kiss me again so I go for it.

Only he was about to say something. Awkwardly, I end up swallowing his words.

By his grip on my hips, I'm going to assume he agrees with my suggestion.

Kissing turns to laughter. At least on his part. I lean away to look at him.

"Come on, let's get out of here." He's smiling and bops me on the nose.

Yes!

Operation Mara Fun Zone continues.

I reach for my phone to text Sofie I'm leaving when I realize I have neither my phone nor my coat. Hell, this dress doesn't even have pockets.

"Hold that thought. Don't leave." I press a quick kiss to his cheek and dash back inside the fray.

Revived by the cold air, I no longer feel like hurling and am able to ninja move my way to the bar to find Sofie.

Spotting me, she shouts above the music, "Why are you back? Did you already have sex with him in the alley?"

She's passed tipsy and has reached delusional drunk.

"Shh. I can't leave without my purse and coat."

I'm guessing she approves of this idea because she jumps up and down. Since she's holding my hands, I'm forced to jump . . . or at least bounce along with her.

"I'm so happy for you!" She hugs me. Now we're hugging

and jumping in the middle of the bar.

"Me too!"

Abruptly, she stops and holds my face in her hands. "Be safe. Text me or Nina if you're not coming home tonight. Leave a scarf on your door if you're not alone. Use condoms."

I untangle myself from her hold. "Thanks, Mom."

She pinches and then pats my cheek. "I'm so proud of you."

"Take care of yourself." I hold out my fist for the cheesy bro bump we've been giving each other for longer than I can remember.

Sofie rolls her eyes and bumps my fist. "I'll see you in a few hours. Don't chicken out!"

On my way back to tall, dark, and orally gifted, I worry he won't be waiting for me. Someone offers me a shot and I take it, not questioning the who or what.

I exhale a relieved breath when I spot his dark hair over the crowd waiting in line.

His face lights up in a grin when our eyes lock. For a second I think about repeating the epic jump from earlier, but don't want to jinx ourselves.

Some things you can't repeat no matter how hard you try.

THREE

MARA

I BLINK AND realize we've survived the mogul strewn cliff. The snow beneath our skis flattens out into a gentle incline.

"Think you can handle this part on your own?" Jesse still skis in front of me.

"French fries and pizza slices. Got it." My lips attempt a smile while my mind shouts memories of our night together. Bending my knees, I enjoy the wind cooling the embarrassed blush on my face. Soon enough he catches up and skis parallel with me.

"Want to race, Doc?" He crouches down and speeds past me. When I don't bite, he slows and waits for me. "Too soon?"

I don't know if he means the nickname or skiing, so I remain silent.

"You okay? Are you having another panic attack? We can slow down." He executes a wide snow plow and falls behind.

I keep up my steady pace. Eyes focused ahead.

He's being charming while I'm hoping for a yeti to pop out from behind a tree and carry me away from this nightmare.

I exhale with relief when we round a corner and the ski lift comes into view.

Until I realize the two of us will be sharing a seat.

"I'm fine now. You're relieved of your duties. Thanks for saving me from death." I give him a gloved thumbs-up.

He chuckles as he gives me a little push forward to catch the next seat. "I'm nothing if not thorough. I'll make sure you get back to the village in one piece."

I twist to catch the seat as it swings behind us. I land in the middle, right up against Jesse's side. Before I can scoot over, we're airborne and he's pulling the safety bar across us. Groaning, I close my eyes.

"You don't have a fear of heights do you?" He touches my hand that's gripping the seat between us.

"A little bit, but I'll be fine."

"Fern didn't like the lifts at first either. Now she's a pro, hopping on and off on her own."

He basically schooled me with his dog. Some women might find it to be insulting, but I typically prefer dogs to people.

"She sounds amazing. You'd never get Tapper on a ski lift."

"He's your dog?"

"He is. Along with Tapper the brown dog, I have two ginger cats. Fred got out in the snow once and you should've seen the look of horror on his face. He didn't speak to me for days and left a hairball on my bed. At least I think it was Fred. George often frames him for bad stuff."

"And you know this how?"

"I've caught George in the act. He pretends he doesn't see me and goes about his criminal affairs like a Boston mobster flaunting the FBI."

"Clearly he's above the law."

"Most definitely." I feel my shoulders relax thinking about my cats. It's true pets are good for relaxation and blood pressure.

"How are you on the dismount?" Jesse points ahead to the end of the ski lift.

Inhaling a steady breath, I fake a smile. "I'll be thrilled with the bronze."

He presses his lips together, making his dimple appear. For some reason, I'm tempted to poke it. Maybe I did that night and can't remember. The whole evening is fuzzy between the time he carried me outside and when I woke up alone the next morning.

He must be terrible in bed if he didn't leave an impression.

Sad, because he's cute and seems nice.

He likes dogs. He's adventurous. Or at least I assume he is by his job. No desk job or ties for him. Tall. Athletic. Enough of a manwhore he doesn't remember sleeping with me.

"Okay, when I jump, you jump. Got it?" He lifts the bar above our heads.

"We're lemmings. Got it."

He barks out a short chuckle. "Ready?"

The chair swings to the top and he bounces off the seat, smoothly gliding out of the way of the chair.

I follow a second later, far less graceful. Recovering by flailing my poles, I ski past him and slow to a stop.

"Thanks for the help. I'll be fine now. I promise." I give him another thumbs-up with my bulky gloves and ski off to the right.

I hear his laugh but I don't turn around. "You're going the wrong way."

It's then I notice I'm going uphill instead of down. I stop the fight and slide backward.

"Right."

He comes up beside me and grins. "You're not getting rid of me so easily."

Of course not. I'm not that lucky.

I peer into the trees, searching for my yeti lover to save me.

Turning around, we head downhill—a very steep, not so friendly hill.

He glides past me. "I might've lied about it all being easy

runs. Come on, Doc, you can do it."

I glare at his swishing skis and long legs.

Stupid, baggy ski pants hiding the good stuff.

I follow him through the trees and keep my skis in his tracks. I'm the duckling to his duck. Every once in a while he turns his head to check on me, giving me a grin of encouragement.

As soon as he faces forward, I stick my tongue out at him. Being mad he doesn't remember me feels better than being embarrassed I'm not memorable.

Maybe he was drunker than me that night and blacked out. He probably has memory issues from a lack of oxygen spending all his time on the mountain. He's probably not that smart.

He's so terrible in bed I've blocked it out.

I don't even remember the good parts, so they must've sucked.

I wish I could remember to know for sure.

We reach an intersection of runs and the quad up to Sam's Knob, which sounds dirtier than it is.

"Should I bother saying I can handle it from here?" I ski parallel to him.

He flips up his goggles. "My shift ends in twenty minutes. Unless someone breaks a leg or tears their ACL, you're stuck with me. I'll drop you off, take the lift back up to the patrol shack, and ski down. Sounds to me like the perfect way to end the day."

"Fine."

He cuts to the left and I follow, thinking he's going to take me down another black run to boost my confidence.

How wrong I was.

He's brought me to the kids' ski area. We're surrounded by toddlers and small humans on skis. Several little girls recognize him and pizza slice their way over in our direction.

Baby ski bunnies. They start them young here.

"Hey, Donna," he greets the instructor by name. She's a frigging ChapStick ad come to life with her blond braids, boobs, and the super white teeth she flashes at him.

"See you on the deck in an hour?" she asks, managing to look and sound innocent and sexy simultaneously.

"Of course. One more run and I'm through. Early shift, no afternoon sweeps for me today."

"I'll save you a seat!"

I catch him shaking his head. "You should join us. Meet some more locals."

"I don't want to be a third wheel."

"Hardly. Après is more like a school bus."

True to his word, he drops me off at the village mall and points out the deck where everyone meets for post-ski drinks and partying.

"Save us a table." He speeds up and disappears down the mountain before I can tell him no.

I debate taking the shuttle home as I click off my skis. The sun is strong and the cloudless sky means sitting on the deck will be warm. *I could use some extra vitamin D*, I tell myself as I spot a family leaving a four top. The nice thing to do would be to save the table for Jesse and his friends. As a thank you. Once he shows up, I can leave and be on my way home.

To my wicked cats.

And Tapper, the three-footed wonder dog.

Not three-legged. He has all four legs, but lost his back left paw as a puppy. Best idea of what happened is he got it stuck in a door. Or some evil human slammed it in a door. A simple amputation and he's been as good as gold ever since. Now he's about four years old. With his flat brown coat and soulful dark eyes, he could be anything from a lab to a boxer mix.

I pull out my phone to check the time. I've only been gone two hours.

Tapper will be fine for another couple of hours without being let out. He's the man in charge of the house and will keep the cats from executing their plans of mass destruction. One time I came home to my apartment and he'd locked them both in the bathroom. I'm still not sure how he managed to get the dynamic duo of evil in there and shut the door behind them, but he stood guard, smugly thumping his tail.

He's a true wonder dog.

I pull up the video app and switch it on. Whoever created nanny and security cameras probably didn't imagine us crazy pet people would use them to spy on our fur babies while we're away.

The living room camera shows Tapper snoozing on the back of the sofa in a pool of sunshine. My sweet boy.

Fred is sitting in the kitchen sink.

Please don't let him be using it as a litter box.

I make a note to buy bleach on my way home.

No sign of George.

I flip to the bedroom camera.

Nothing.

Switching back to the living room, I shriek. A close up of George's anus greets me, up close and personal.

My cat is mooning me.

"That little fu—" I fumble my phone while trying to close the app.

"This seat free?"

I blink up at the voice. A Norse god stands before me, gesturing to one of my coveted empty chairs.

"—cker," I finish swearing about George. The word comes out sounding like sure.

"Thanks." I expect him to hoist the chair above his head and take it with him back to wherever he came from, but he surprises me by sitting down. "Are you waiting for friends?"

"Um," I pause, not sure if I would call Jesse a friend or not, "yes?"

Why am I asking him?

"Not sure if you're meeting people? Or not sure if they're friends?" He smiles at a few people walking into the beer garden.

"The latter. We just met."

"Traveling alone?" His voice sounds like maple syrup poured on snow—smooth and sweet.

"No. I live here."

Tall, blond, and smooth studies me. "You do? I haven't seen you around before. I know most of the locals. I'm Landon."

"Mara. Nice to meet you." I reach across the table to shake his hand. "Unless you have pets or are in the market to adopt, you've probably missed me. I work at Hawks Creek Ranch."

"Sage's thing?" His cheerful smile falters slightly.

"Elizabeth Hawks runs it, but Sage Blum is on the board, if that's what you mean."

"That's the place. What do you do there?" He leans closer and I get a whiff of his cologne. Cologne for a day of skiing strikes me as a little odd, but maybe he freshened up for après ski?

"I'm the staff veterinarian." I can't keep the pride out of my voice. Nearly a decade after announcing I was going to college to become a vet, I've finally achieved my goal.

Norseman gives me an appreciative nod. "We should toast to that."

He waves over the waitress and orders beer along with a mix of appetizers. I guess he plans to hang out for a while.

"And for you?" The waitress gives me the once over.

I'm suddenly self-conscious about the size of my pom-pom. I hum as I think of what to order. "I'm not much of a beer drinker."

"What do you like? Lager? Porter? Stout? Ale?"

Honestly, the only time I've drank beer was out of kegs at college parties. And back then, the beer tasted like socks and stale corn nuts. "I don't know."

"Bring her the Blue Moon," my new Viking friend suggests. "It comes with an orange slice as a garnish, so it's kind of like a cocktail."

"Okay." I'm relieved he ordered for me, saving me from asking for a Coors Light, the only beer I remember is from Colorado. And only because my dad's favorite joke about me moving out here is getting fresh Coors.

I'm not even sure if fresh beer is a thing.

Our drinks arrive, and he holds up his glass. "To new friends."

"To new friends." I clink my glass against his.

I'm relieved I like mine. Not a whiff of old corn nuts or sweaty socks. The orange is a nice touch. Makes drinking seem healthy. Like how sangria is healthier for us because it's a giant fruit cocktail. Or how potato vodka counts as a vegetable.

"Good?"

Smiling, I nod.

"I knew you'd like it." His lips curve into a smug smirk.

Is it the pom-pom? I take off my hat and set it on an empty chair. My hair springs back to life after I run my hands through the roots at the crown. The joy of curly hair.

"How?" I clear my throat. "We met five minutes ago."

"It's my superpower." He winks at me, and I'm reminded of Gilderoy Lockhart in Harry Potter. Landon thinks highly of himself and his charms.

"Have you worked as a bartender?"

He scoffs with a frown. "No, bartending is for losers."

Pretty rude words given we're in a bar right now.

"What do you do for a living?"

My question is drowned out by a series of whoops from a trio of guys high-fiving him from the other side of the barricade separating the sun deck from the slope. Two of them hop the barrier when the table behind Landon opens up. Never mind if there's a wait for tables, they claim it as their own. They shift chairs around to create a longer table with ours.

Landon doesn't introduce me. I wait for him to make introductions, but give up after a few awkward moments. Instead, I smile and sip my beer while people watching.

By people and watching I mean I'm staring at the crowd waiting for Jesse to show up.

FOUR

JESSE

THE RADIO SQUAWKS to life with a report of a woman sitting down on the final section of Powderhorn.

"I've got it," I respond and grab my skis.

Outside the ski patrol shack, I go into autopilot as I ski down the upper part of the run. I grew up in these mountains and could probably ski with my eyes closed. Not something I'd recommend anyone do.

The whole point is to not over think.

Focus on what's happening now.

Get the job finished and move on.

Always be in control.

I could be referring to skiing. Or my job.

Hell, anything in my life.

Ever since Cody.

Out of the three brothers, I'm the only one still living here. Aspen's silver town saloons and honky-tonks are long gone, but the craving for wealth is alive and well in the Roaring Fork Valley. Instead of prospectors mining for their share of the silver, now the town is filled with capitalists who made their fortunes elsewhere. The town still makes it easy to spend money and flaunt wealth.

If that's your thing and helps you sleep better at night.

For us regular folks who live in the valley, it's kind of a pain in the ass.

Good luck finding affordable housing.

Looking for a cheap place to rent? Don't think about the trailer park in Woody Creek. It's out of your price range.

Most regular folks live down valley. Where the mountains are still as pretty but the air is less rarified.

We try not to let reality spoil the illusion.

Gingerbread cottages sell for millions. So do fractional ownerships of condos. Want a week or two a year of the good life? It'll cost you.

Living in paradise isn't cheap.

Most of us work a couple of jobs depending on the season.

Ski patrol in the winter, maybe construction in the summer. Or bartender. Or retail.

We do it because we feel itchy over the thought of living anywhere else.

My brain feels heavy at sea level. The real world stands on my chest, full of oxygen and bad memories.

I prefer to stay at high altitude and away from the city.

Chasing fame, power, or money has never appealed to me.

I've seen firsthand what it does to people.

I chatter away while I ski Mara down to the chair lift even though I'm pretty sure she's not listening. Probably in shock from the panic attack, she stares straight ahead most of the run, only making eye contact a few times.

She's not a bad skier. In fact, she could've made it down the rest of the run on her own with more confidence and a little guidance.

After dropping off Mara, I speed down to the base village to catch the high speed six pack back to the patrol shack. As I pass the beer garden, I catch myself scanning the crowd for her ridiculous hat. When I see she's found a table, I smile. Until I see she's sitting with Landon Roberts.

What the actual fuck?

My smile dies on my face. The happy bubble I'd been in since finding Mara bursts.

It can't be ten minutes from when I left her until now.

The man is a master at the pick-up, but this has to be a new record for even him.

"What an asshole."

"Mom, he said a bad word."

I forgot I'm sitting on a lift with a kid.

Cursing in my uniform. Great.

"I said, 'Look a castle.'" I point down to the snow sculptures on the side of Fanny Hill.

"I don't see it." The kid wiggles around.

"Hey, hold still, little guy. We're kind of high up and it's a long way down." I brace my arm across his chest to get him to settle. Over his head, I mouth "sorry" at his mother.

"He hears a lot worse from his father." She lifts her goggles and gives me the once over.

Cougar alert, Village Express lift. Patroller trapped.

"Diesel, do you want to ask the nice patrolman any questions?" she asks him while still undressing me with her eyes.

Diesel? People name their kids weird things.

"What's your name?" he asks, swinging his pint-sized skis.

Start at the basics. Good move, kid. "Jesse."

His mom giggles softly. "Do you have a girl?"

Enough with the Springfield jokes.

Yes, we all know the song.

Yes, my name is Jesse.

Believe it or not, I have heard this all before.

Like my entire life.

Sorry, you're not original.

Better luck next time.

Considering my brothers got named Wyatt and Cody, I lucked out with Jesse. My dad had a thing for Westerns. Maybe because the good guys always won. Simpler, more straight forward times.

"No, ma'am." I hope the ma'am conveys my polite disinterest. She's nice, pretty even, but I'm not interested. I focus on Diesel, pointing out the various runs we can see from the lift. I'm using her own kid to block her advances. A few more minutes and I'll be free.

Okay, here's the deal.

Women like vacation sex.

Do I have a scientific study to back up this fact? No.

What I do have is a firsthand knowledge from every man I know in the greater Roaring Fork Valley.

It's one of the biggest perks of life in a resort town.

A constant supply of women on vacation looking for the kind of local color that doesn't hang in one of Aspen's many art galleries.

One of the best parts of living in a ski town is never having to face your one-night stand again once her weekend or ski week is over. Or at least not until next season. By then, a forgetful mind and a vague, friendly smile can ease many an awkward situation when you can't remember the name or the face, but you recognize the familiar look in her eyes. Sometimes it says she's up for another round. Sometimes there's shame.

Listen to me, life's too short for shame.

Own your impulses.

Maybe the lack of oxygen at high altitude can be blamed for stronger Jell-O shots and lowered inhibitions.

Maybe it's the charm of the local mountain men.

Best not to analyze it too closely.

If it works, don't tinker.

We're all consenting adults here.

Well, except for Fern. She's only two and a half. In dog years, she's still a teenager.

She's the best girl a guy could have. Doesn't stop her from being a pain in my ass, but at least I know she loves me unconditionally. Trust me, she's the only bitch I'll ever put up with.

Life's too short for strings and attachments.

Might sound harsh, but we all know what we're doing here. Consenting adults who right swipe the moment.

Don't call us sluts or manwhores. Most of us are nice guys.

And if we're not, does it matter if you'll never see us again?

Aspen during ski season is Tinder in real life.

Hell, in Snowmass we even have a run called Grinder, although I'm pretty sure it predates the app.

Part of the joys of being a vacation hook up is avoiding the awkwardness of seeing each other again.

Unless we're part of the monogamy brigade, who pair off like it hasn't stopped raining for over thirty days and the bearded guy down valley is building an ark.

The rest of us run in a wolf pack, sticking together, watching each other's backs.

I never take advantage of a girl who's too drunk or too high.

I'm not an asshole.

Some guys are. As long as a woman is conscious and breathing, they don't see a problem.

The things I've heard bragged about in the patrol shack or after a rugby match make me want to punch something. Or someone.

I've never had a black book or notches in my headboard, but if I've slept with a woman, I remember. At least her face.

I'm typically excellent with faces. Names are tougher to remember.

Mara looked familiar to me, but I can't place her.

I'm ninety-five percent certain I've never seen her naked. Or had sex with her.

I'd remember.

I'm sure of it.

Even during my wildest days with Cody, I never forgot a woman I had sex with.

Kissed? Hell, that was another story.

When he was around, women threw themselves at anything with testosterone within his general vicinity. Kind of like jumping into one of those ball pits, and about as sanitary.

Being part of his posse meant always being a runner up or honorable mention, but still got me laid.

Thanks, little brother.

After being the first off the lift, I give Diesel a friendly wave and a smile to his mom before skiing over to the shack. A pair of rescue toboggans rest against the wall where we also park the snowmobiles.

Okay, it's nicer than a true shack, but not by much. Ski patrol has several of these buildings on each mountain. This outpost is typical of the bunch. Brown wood siding and big picture windows cover the exterior. Nothing fancy. There's a ramp to the front door. Inside is the operations office, a locker room, kitchen, and a lounge with a wood stove. Basic.

Throughout the day, the rooms will fill and empty with employees. It always smells like coffee, ramen noodles, wet GORE-TEX, and woodsmoke. There really isn't a decor, other than clutter. Boots, parkas, hats, and gloves fill lockers and spill on the floor. Old ski posters cover the walls and ceiling. The break room counters hold cups of soup, hot chocolate packets, and enough mugs for an army. Basically, anything you can eat or drink with just water and heat. Packs, emergency kits, and medical supplies line the shelves opposite the kitchen area. Behind a locked door live the explosives and other equipment for avalanches.

Nothing about the space is glamorous or charming, but it's the heart and pulse of the mountain.

Without us, there'd be no happy skiers.

We break up fights.

We save the drunks from themselves.

Break a bone, we'll get you to medical help.

Lose your way, we'll find you.

Freak out, we'll talk you down.

I open the front door and whistle. Fern comes bounding out of the lounge area. She stretches in front of me. Her eyes are sleepy.

"You and Zane have a good afternoon?" Fern's boyfriend, Zane, a black lab, is another ski patrol dog. They spend their downtime snuggled on an old recliner near the fire.

It's a rough life.

Earlier today we had an avalanche drill. To the dogs, it's a big game of hide and seek. When Fern first started her training, we hid her favorite toy in the snow. Now we hide a human in a hole and she finds us. Same game to her, with a bigger reward.

I hope we never have to put her training into action, but I know if we do, she'll do her best.

Fern wags her tail and stands up to get her ears scratched.

"Ready to clock out?" I ask, giving her a chest rub.

She replies with an enthusiastic bark.

Like me, she wears a patrol uniform. I remove her working vest and hang it up next to my gear in my cubby. Finding my name magnet on the board, I slide it to the "off duty" area.

I wave to Nic in dispatch on my way out the door.

"Good work today," she says as I pass. Pretty sure she says the same thing to me every day we work together.

Outside I bump into Abe and Johan, two of our most senior patrollers. While Abe is craggy and bearded, tall and broad, Johan stands five foot eight in his socks and resembles a blond otter with his large eyes and slim build. Both men are in their early fifties and have spent over half their lives on these mountains. Talk about life goals, I want to be them when I grow up.

"Be well," I say as I put on my skis.

"We're going to be doing some blasting tomorrow," Abe says. "Be sure to get here early if you want to be on the team."

He knows full well I won't miss it. "I'll start the coffee for you in the morning."

First one to arrive always starts the coffeemaker. The inside joke is Abe and Johan have never made a pot of coffee in their twenty-plus years on the mountain.

I pat my chest. Fern takes a running leap, lands on my thigh, and then bounces up to my shoulder. I scoop her into position. Sometimes I let her run between my skis, but it's the end of the day. We'll get down the mountain quicker if I carry her.

A silly pom-pom flashes into my head followed by Mara's laugh.

I know that laugh from before today.

A certainty hits me square in the chest.

We've met before.

The details are still fuzzy, but now I'm ninety-nine percent sure we've never had sex.

I'm sure I'd remember.

My number isn't that high I wouldn't. Or can't.

She didn't say anything.

Maybe she doesn't remember me.

Or maybe she forgot me on purpose.

Neither of those options put a smile on my face.

Both of them pretty much suck.

The when, where, how of our first meeting doesn't come to me, but now I'm a man with a plan to remember.

FIVE

MARA

LANDON HOLDS COURT at our table. Apparently, he knows everyone on the mountain, waving and smiling in greeting to new arrivals. One time, he even winks and gives someone the double thumbs-up like a slimy movie politician. I don't really say much, but he fills the gaps in conversation with local gossip and trivia. The man gives excellent floor show.

Currently, he's telling me about Ted Bundy's infamous courthouse escape and my mind begins comparing him to classic serial killer profiles. He ticks off a lot of the key profile traits: intelligent, self-assured, and charming.

I'm not saying he *is* a serial killer. Or a psychopath. Or even a sociopath. Of course not. He's the one who brought up the subject.

Just saying he is a charming charmer.

Movement out of the corner of my eye catches my attention. Jesse swooshes to a stop near the ski rack. He's carrying a dog on his shoulders.

There's a dog hanging out on his shoulder like it's totally comfortable and normal. In fact, the dog looks like she's smiling—huge grin on her face. Can you blame her?

Let's slow down and rewind this scene, shall we?

Tall, dark, and rugged man skies down the mountain with a dog on his shoulders.

I'm not sure I've ever seen anything more sexy.

The fluffy brown dog, who I assume is Fern, jumps down when they come to a stop. Her whole body wiggles as she wags her tail in joy.

Happy dog is happy.

I'd be wagging my tail if I were her, too. When he joked about carrying me down the mountain, I didn't take him seriously. Sadly, I don't think him carrying me would be nearly as adorable. Or sexy.

I press my lips together to keep my jaw from hanging open. Or drooling. Reminding myself he didn't remember me, I attempt to calm the racing of my heart.

He's no longer wearing his ski patrol parka. Instead, he's switched to a mossy green fleece and a gray beanie, but unfortunately, he's still wearing the same ski pants.

He sees me and waves, stomping toward the deck in his boots, Fern following close behind.

Two women at the table next to me loudly sigh. *Or maybe it was me.*

"How do you know Jesse?" My new buddy Landon watches Jesse weave his way through the growing crowd to our table.

"We met on the mountain today." I leave out the near-death experience.

And the one-night stand two years ago.

"Doc, you did good." Jesse stops at the end of our table. Fern jumps up and puts her feet on the edge. "Bad manners, Fern."

She glances up at him and hops down.

"Good girl." Smiling, he pats her head.

I catch myself grinning at the two of them and their cuteness.

"This is Fern. She'll give you a proper shake if you ask her."

"Nice to meet you, Fern." I hold out my hand. "Shake."

She gives me her paw in greeting.

"She's normally well behaved, but we're working on her crowd skills." Jesse's smile dies as he stares at the Viking sitting across from me. "Landon."

"Hayes." Landon gives him one of those classic bro nods. Neither men smiles in greeting.

Interesting.

Jesse sits in the chair beside mine. I feel Fern squeeze between our legs and lie near my feet. I can't resist reaching down to pet her thick brown fur.

"Slumming in Snowmass today?" Jesse's tone is colder than the water dripping off the icicles hanging from the roof as he addresses Landon. He seemed friendly earlier, but his frown is anything but warm.

"Heard your mom was skiing Fanny Hill today."

"Really, Roberts? A mom joke?" Jesse leans closer to me. "Is he bothering you?"

"We were having a fine time until you showed up," Landon answers for me.

"I was holding the table and he asked if the seat was free." I smile, always the peacemaker. "Kept me from ordering an old corn nut beer."

While Landon makes a face, Jesse laughs. "Not quite the same as saving a life, but I guess you gotta do what you can."

His barb hits its target. Landon mumbles something that sounds like "asshole" under his breath.

Apparently, I've landed in the middle of an ongoing war. Maybe Jesse and I should find another table. I scan the area for an empty spot. The crowd has grown to be standing room only and several people are dancing in the narrow space between tables and the bar.

"So," I take a sip of beer and try to think of something

neutral to say, "You two know each other?"

"We do," Jesse replies.

"For years," Landon adds.

Clearly, they're BFFs. I wonder which one has the "Be Fri" side of the split heart pendant and which one is "st ends."

"We've played in the same rugby club for a few summers." Jesse flags the waitress to order a beer. "You okay or you need a refill?"

I examine my beer. The glass is definitely more than half full. "I'm good."

He doesn't ask Landon if he needs anything.

"Rugby. Wow." I know nothing about rugby. Soccer, lacrosse, and way too much about football, but rugby is as foreign to me as if he said they jousted or played cricket together. I think only the British do any of those sports, although I'm not sure if jousting is popular with kids today. "Cool."

"You a fan?" Landon asks.

"Can't say I am. Never watched it."

"You should come to our matches this summer. Or at least show up for Rugbyfest in September. Best weekend of the year." There's a certain smugness about Landon. Unless he doesn't own a mirror, he has to know he's good looking. In fact, he might even be arrogant about it.

Unlike Jesse. He's more unassuming, which makes him even sexier. Jesse's hair is untamed, messy waves, whereas Landon is neatly groomed and looks like he uses a lot of styling products.

Mountain man versus well groomed Viking.

Life is full of difficult decisions.

The arrival of our appetizer bonanza breaks the mounting tension between the two guys. I'm happy to stuff fries in my mouth to avoid more tense conversation. Instead, I people watch.

Most of our fellow patrons sport variations of ski garb.

Lift tickets dangle from the zippers of more North Face and Bogner jackets than I've ever seen in one place. The men are almost uniformly handsome and the women are beautiful. Fit, healthy, and rosy-cheeked, this crowd is in the top percentile of humans who are not actual supermodels.

Except the two women in furry hats and matching fur boots to their knees. I'm pretty sure they are actual supermodels. Or clones of Giselle.

Donna from the kids' ski area joins us along with a couple of other guys from ski patrol. They magically find more chairs. We shift around to create enough room for everyone.

I forget most of the other names as soon as people say them. One of my weird ticks. Animal names I always remember. People? Usually I remember faces, or their pet's name, but not theirs.

I sip another beer, keeping my wits and pants about my person. Altitude still affects how quickly I go from personably tipsy to drunk girl.

And no one wants to be the drunk girl.

Landon leaves the group first, claiming other plans. He and I are the only two who don't work for the ski company and I get the feeling he's on the outs with most of the other guys.

Before he goes, he pays our original tab, which is totally unnecessary but very sweet. He stands and then steps closer to me. Resting a hand on my shoulder, he dips his head down so only I can hear his voice below the din of the crowd.

"It was great to meet you, Mara. Perhaps next time we'll be able to get to know each other better without the big entourage."

A shiver runs over my skin when he squeezes the fleshy part of my upper arm. Part of me is turned on by his words and the not-so-thinly-veiled sexual overtone. Another part of me still thinks about Ted Bundy's handsome face.

"Okay. Great." I'm not sure what I'm saying. I've never been so close to a Norse warrior before.

"It's a small town. I'm sure we'll see each other soon." He gives my arm another squeeze before he disappears into the crowd.

"I thought he'd never leave." Jesse leans closer to me. "Watch out for him."

Something about his warning rubs me the wrong way. Like he's in any position to be giving out warnings about other guys? He's probably the biggest rapscallion in the entire valley. Ski patrol. Dog. Rugged good looks. Dangerous. He's a living, breathing double-black diamond.

He's a walking GQ . . . no, Men's Health, cover model.

He's horrible.

I lean away from him. "Thanks for the advice."

He blinks at me, then his gaze wanders to my lips as his brow furrows. "You're welcome." Not sure why he sounds confused.

Unless he caught the sarcasm in my tone. I'm not always as subtle as I think I am.

The sun dips behind the slopes and the outdoor heaters turn on as the golden hour ends.

I say my good-byes to the group at large and turn to Jesse. "Thanks again for saving me today. I'd probably still be making my way down on my butt. My non-frozen butt and I thank you."

What am I even saying? I need to stop talking.

"I'm here to protect and serve. Safety first, non-frozen asses second." He gives me a genuine smile with full dimple.

Fern jumps into my empty chair. I'm pretty sure she's breaking some sort of health-code rule, but who am I to judge. "Nice to meet you, too."

She bumps my hand with her cold nose.

"If you ever need anything, bring her by the ranch. I owe you one."

"Nah, we're even. Just another day on the mountain." His smile fades slightly. "Nice to meet you, Mara."

"You too, Jesse." I force my own smile to be brighter.

Walking away, I curse his friendly professionalism and poor memory.

It's a small town. I'm sure we'll run into each other again. Over and over. Help! How will I avoid him forever?

I remind myself the local motto seems to be out of sight, out of mind.

As I wait for the shuttle, I make plans to only ski at Buttermilk Mountain for the rest of the season.

SIX

JESSE

A FEW DAYS later, I stop at the ski shop in the village on my way to the shuttle. It's been snowing on and off all day. We need the fresh snow, but people expect clear skies and sunshine when they come to Colorado to ski. The mountain's filled with cranky skiers when it snows. Makes patrolling less fun when everyone wants to complain about the weather.

Believe it or not, the ski company doesn't control Mother Nature. I'm sure upper management has people working on a plan to change that. For now we're stuck. Yes, we can make snow overnight, but we can't stop the real stuff from falling during the day.

I stomp through the door, still in my boots and not caring if I track wet snow behind me.

Rick's behind the counter, ringing up a sale when he spots me. "Hayes, what can I do for you?"

"I need a helmet." I eye the selection on the wall behind him.

He finishes up with the customer before focusing on me. "For yourself?"

"No, I'm all set. It's for . . ." A friend? Are we friends? I'm not sure I'd go as far as saying Mara and I are buddies. "Mara

Keiley, the new vet down at Elizabeth's ranch."

"Yeah, I've seen her around. About this tall," he holds his hand to his shoulder, "and curvy?"

Annoyed at his conspiratorial bro wink, I stop him before he completes an imaginary hourglass with his hands. "Yes, her. How many new veterinarians moved here recently?"

"Only her as far as I know." Rick sounds confused.

"Then show some respect and not focus on her body."

He gives me a sidelong stare. "Okay then. Dr. Keiley needs a ski helmet and you're here to buy her one? Just so I'm clear."

"It's a welcome present."

"Ski patrol is handing out free helmets to new residents?"

"Not officially."

With narrowed eyes, he resembles a brown weasel. A weasel with a little hairy nub on top of his head. Whatever he's got going on up there isn't enough to make a bun and he should give up the fight.

I huff. "Quit staring at me. I'm buying her a helmet because she doesn't have one."

"Safety first?" He smirks.

"Always."

"What you see is what I have in stock. You want something else, I'll have to do a special order. We're out of a lot of things after the holidays."

I examine the display. Black and white are the standard, but women's helmets come in pink, red, turquoise, blue . . . too many damn choices.

Her beanie is red, so she probably likes the color.

"Give me the Giro in red."

"What size?"

"What's a normal size for a woman's head?"

"Normal? They vary. She's kind of petite, but she has a lot of hair."

"You're not really helping here." I'm annoyed he seems to know a lot of details about her.

"Buy the medium. If it doesn't fit, she can always bring it back and we'll exchange it."

I have zero experience buying girl stuff. Is this one of those situations where if I get the size wrong, she'll be insulted I'm saying she has a big head? It's a helmet. Not lingerie.

"Fine, let's go with that one."

"Want me to gift wrap it?" He grins at me.

"Since when do you wrap ski equipment?"

"I'm sure I have a box and a bow around here somewhere. Since it's a special gift for a special lady."

I silence him with a glare. "Stay out of it."

"You doing Power this year?" He changes the subject.

"Probably. You?"

"No way, man. I only ski down the mountain unless I'm climbing Buttermilk during a full moon night."

"Power's no joke."

Every February racers traverse all four mountains in the area and a lot of it involves uphilling. Rick's right. It's a nightmare unless you're crazy.

Like me.

Ski patrol usually pulls together a couple of teams. I haven't missed a race in four years.

Rick, being the asshole he is, slaps a huge bow on the helmet before slipping it into a bag. "Tell Dr. Keiley hello."

"Fuck off." I bristle at his teasing and fake formality. "Tell her yourself. Or better yet, don't."

His laughter echoes outside the store after I exit.

It's *only* a helmet for a new resident who thinks a beanie and a pom-pom will magically protect her head from more than the cold.

While tens of thousands of people come to the mountains

for ski season, it's a rare event when a person moves here permanently. Or as permanent as living in a resort town can be. I can't tell you the number of people, both men and women, I've met over the years who live here for a season and move on. Some return for a couple of years in a row. Not many. Life here can sometimes feel like living year round at a summer camp. The campers come and go, taking their happy memories of fun times with them. We stay behind and enjoy the quiet in-between seasons.

Fern and I make the short drive home. She does a quick perimeter loop to make sure her property remained safe during her absence before scratching at the back door to come inside.

While I make dinner, Fern lies on her mat, patiently waiting for her own meal. I enjoy the silence only interrupted by the sound of a knife against a wooden chopping board and the sizzle of chicken cooking in the cast iron dutch oven on the gas stove. The repetition of my actions creates a meditative state, allowing me to reflect on my day on the mountain.

Some days are tougher to process than others, especially if there's been a severe injury or a death. Thankfully, those events are rare.

My gaze catches on a family photo from ten years ago stuck to the fridge with a magnet. In it, all three of the Hayes boys smile for the camera on top of a snowy peak. Not quite kids, not yet men. Cody stands in the middle, his arms lovingly holding Wyatt and I in headlocks. He always had to be the center of attention.

Tucked behind the picture is a prayer card of Jesus holding a lamb.

In my head, I can hear Cody asking if he's supposed to be the lamb or Jesus.

In spite of the dull ache in my chest, I chuckle.

My green chile chicken simmers in the same pan my

grandmother used to make hers. I use her recipe and somehow it never tastes the same if I don't make it in her old pan, too.

I know Inez still watches over her boys. She always told us she'd keep an eye on us no matter what. Then she'd pinch our cheeks hard enough to make her words sound like a warning.

From an old Colorado ranch family, my mother taught us to believe in hard work and simple living. When houses started disrupting their view of the mountains, my parents bought more acreage down valley and moved to Carbondale. Dad said he was tired of fighting celebrities and "millionaires with more money than humanity" for a table to eat ribs at his favorite barbecue joint in Aspen. Now he complains about Walmart underselling the local merchants and how much he has to pay for decent beef at Whole Foods.

At least Mom still makes homemade tortillas for me. I pull a couple of them out of the freezer to have with my chicken. The last two dozen of her Christmas tamales sits forlornly on the shelf next to a pint of triple chocolate gelato. I always save some tamales until at least summer even if they get freezer burned because my mother, like her mother Inez, refuses to make them any other time of the year besides the big tamale day before Christmas Eve.

As my dinner cooks, I fill a bowl of kibble for Fern. We have a routine of tricks she performs before she can eat. With a sassy bark, she follows my commands: shake, high five, spin, figure eight through my legs, and a return to her mat. I release her to eat and she gives me a final bark telling me exactly what she thinks of my silly demands.

My phone lights up with text messages inviting me out, encouraging me to join the fun in Aspen. Ski season can be one long party if you want, especially during the annual X Games at Buttermilk.

These days I prefer to work on projects around my house,

spend time with Fern, and get used to a new normal without Cody. Life may be a party, but sometimes not showing up is the best way to survive. Fern might be a professional avalanche dog, but it's my life she saved two years ago after Cody died.

When Willow calls in a favor for tomorrow night, I say yes without hesitating. Making up for the sins of my brother seems the least I can do. Our family shares her heartbreak and betrayal. Cody didn't only leave her in a pile of shattered dreams, he did the same thing to us.

We're comrades from the same battle.

Tomorrow is a fundraiser for some celebrity charity loosely tied to the X games. There's been talk of starting a foundation in Cody's name, but it feels too soon.

Not sure what cause a charity with his name would benefit.

Arrogant assholes who think they're immortal?

Cocky bastards who do stupid shit and die?

SEVEN

MARA

MY MOM ALWAYS says life is what happens when your dishes are piling up in the sink.

If that's true, then my empty sink and dishwasher tell a sad tale.

Life on the ranch is beautiful, but quiet.

I'm grateful to have the apartment in the converted barn as part of my contract. I'd never be able to afford to rent at the market rate without a long commute. One of the board members, Sage Blum, donated money last year to hire a full-time vet and also build out the hayloft into a second floor apartment for said person. Elizabeth Hawks, the ranch owner, lives in a small house across the property. She's lovely, but also my boss. I can't show up every night for dinner like a stray.

I'm extremely grateful to Elizabeth for hiring me. There's no way I'm the most qualified applicant, but not everyone would be willing to accept a lower salary and live in a converted barn above a bunch of pygmy goats and a donkey named Pacey.

This apartment isn't a forever situation, but a much better option than a third floor walk-up outside of Boston that smells of hot dogs and musty closets.

Outside the window over the sink, my view extends east down into a sweeping valley lined with rosy-red tinged hills. Both the bedroom and living room face west and the spectacular sunsets over snowy peaks. A grove of bare aspen trees stands guard near the main road. I can't wait to see them turn gold in the fall.

Pens for a few of the resident animals cluster together on the southern end of the building.

The whole place is pretty much my idea of heaven. Being surrounded by animals, kind people, and a beautiful landscape is a dream.

Then why am I moping around?

I pick up the journal of veterinary medicine and flip the pages as I sit in the big comfy chair by the window.

I could read up on the latest theriogenolgy case study. Or environmental enrichment for shelter cats.

I could and should.

At the very least I should familiarize myself with the use of propofol in canine general anesthesia.

Wait, isn't propofol the drug that killed Michael Jackson?

I can never remember.

I could probably look it up on my phone, but I judge myself for not remembering these key tidbits of celebrity gossip.

With a sigh, I toss the journal on the table. I need to get off the ranch.

Or just get off.

I need more AA batteries.

The yawning cat on the journal's cover echoes my boredom and lack of sex.

George comes over and sits on the cat's face.

"Don't destroy it before I read about enriching your environment, mister."

I attempt to lift the magazine from beneath him. It goes

about as well as trying to slide leaf from under a boulder.

"That's it. I'm putting you on a diet."

He narrows his green eyes at me. I can't tell if he's calling my bluff or telling me to go ahead and try.

Can cats glower? Where's the unbiased peer reviewed article about smugness in domesticated felines?

Having enough, I decide I'm going to take myself into Aspen for a movie and popcorn with extra butter. Doesn't matter what's playing as long as it isn't an animal movie. I can't stomach those, especially if it's a talking animal movie. Those are the worst.

No cat sounds like Jude Law.

Everyone knows this.

Although I did break this rule for the Jungle Book. Because Idris Elba.

Okay, I also saw the new Tarzan because of Alex Skarsgård.

Who wouldn't make exceptions for those two? I could listen to Idris read me the AVMA journal all day, any day of the week ending in ay.

I let Tapper out for an evening constitutional and feed him, watching as he eats all of his food before George can help himself. I add kibble to the cat bowls and make sure everyone has water. Animals all set, I change into clean jeans and a soft cashmere sweater.

Walking down the stairs, I pull on my knit beanie and coat while I debate driving to the lot at the bottom of the hill and taking the shuttle, or braving Aspen's parking.

I decide to brave the parking roulette. It's a Wednesday. How bad can it be?

Ha.

Until I see all the signage near the airport, I'd forgotten the X games are taking place this week. Traffic creeps past Buttermilk where the games are held until the roundabout. Downtown

Aspen isn't much better.

With all the cool people partying at the bars and clubs, the movie theater should be empty. I park behind the Hotel Jerome and plan to walk back through town to the Isis.

Rounding the corner in front of the hotel, I stumble upon a bank of cameras and one of those logo patterned backdrops celebrities walk in front of at red carpet events.

My curiosity gets the better of me. I glance at my phone. I have a few minutes to gawk at the glam people before the movie starts.

I squeeze in next to two women and watch an elegant couple pose for cameras. Flashes go off like a lightning storm as they smile and turn.

"Who is that?" I ask the middle aged woman and her friend next to me.

They blink at me like I've asked who Santa is.

"That's the couple from the latest season of *In Love with the Bachelor!*" the shorter of the two women answers.

Her friend sighs. "Kyle and Kylie are made for each other."

Okay. I'm sure their TV romance will last a lifetime because they have basically the same name. Meant to be!

An enormous black SUV with tinted windows pulls up to the curb and the squeals from the crowd increase.

"I knew it! I knew it!" Shorter fangirl starts bouncing next to me.

I peer between the crowd of burly paparazzi and excited fan-girls to the other end of the carpet. A beautiful brunette turns to face us. I recognize Willow Cross instantly. She's wearing five sequins held together by a few threads. "She must be freezing."

Sighing woman shoots me a look that tells me I'm ruining the moment. "If you had a body like Willow's, wouldn't you be showing it off too?"

I nod.

Wait a second. Was that an insult?

"Who's she with?" Shorty pushes against me to get a better look.

"No way! It's Jesse Hayes!"

"No way." My words echo hers, but don't hold the same enthusiasm. Why would some random ski patrol guy be on the red carpet? "Who's that?"

"He's Cody Hayes' brother."

I stare at her blankly. "Who?" Maybe Jesse has a twin? I rack my mind for pictures of her and a boyfriend in the tabloids.

"X Games champion?" Her exasperation at my ignorance comes out in a huff. "He's only the greatest extreme winter sports athlete ever."

"Was. It's such a shame what happened." Sigher sighs. "Poor Willow."

Was?

He retired?

Or he's dead?

"Sad, but her and Jesse are totally hot together. I ship them because they're the ultimate love conquers all story." Shorty practically swoons with the story she has going on inside her head about a couple she doesn't even know.

How do I not know Jesse has, had, a famous brother? I'm a celebrity gossip failure to not know Willow was with an athlete. Maybe because I've never followed the X Games? Or I spent most of my twenties in labs and studying?

The urge to stalk the Hayes brothers online grows. With a few swipes and clicks, I could probably find out their entire family saga. And Jesse's dating history, if he's the kind of guy to date celebrities. Which all evidence points to as truth. How did I not know he has a girlfriend? Not that we shared our whole life stories on the mountain last week.

What was he doing slumming with a regular mortal like me?

Maybe he does remember our night together but is too embarrassed to admit he slept with me.

The bastard.

Now I'm pissed. What? I'm not good enough for him?

He's a glorified EMT. I'm a doctor. I perform surgery. I bring life into the world.

I'm a friggin' modern day female Doctor Doolittle.

Except I don't actually talk to the animals and think they talk back.

I'm not crazy.

"I slept with him. He's not all that. Pretty much the opposite of memorable," I blurt out to my new friends.

Okay, I might have to retract the not crazy part.

Sigher and Shorty stare at me like I'm insane.

Clearly, I'm a woman on the edge.

"It's true." I nod. "Not memorable at all."

I sneak a glance at Jesse and his celebrity date as they pose for pictures. What was I thinking? He'd be a normal, regular guy because he works in ski patrol? This is Aspen, where everything that glitters is either gold, diamonds, or platinum.

I'm way out of my league.

As I turn to go, his eyes flash to mine. I see the moment he recognizes me because his brows shoot up. His fake smile falters a second before he recovers and his friendly guy façade slips back into place.

"Ohmygod, he does know you." Sigher pinches my arm hard enough to leave a mark.

"Ouch!" I yelp loudly and two photographers lower their cameras to get a better look at me.

I need to get out of here before my mouth gets me into more trouble. Or Jesse tries to talk to me.

With little resistance, I manage to slip through the crowd and cross the street. Flashes reflect off of the windows of cars I pass.

My thoughts and feelings churn together over tonight's revelation. *Do I want something more with Jesse?* The thought starts a war between my brain and hormones.

Does everyone do an online search of their love interests? Am I the only one not stalking on Google and social media to get the scoop on prospective lovers? Is this normal? What happened to the simple days of love at first sight? Swipe left, swipe right doesn't have the same ring to it. Evidently, even the regular guys around here date super-humans.

I wonder what dating was like during the silver mining days in this town. Did people date? Did they show up with a wife, or wives, in tow? Only pay for sex with the ladies of the evening at the local whorehouses? Sex without strings seems to be the historical tradition.

I don't know why it bothers me so much. Most animals don't pair-bond for life. Talk about sex without emotions. We want to believe in the wolves who mate for life instead of accepting the reality that infidelity happens in almost half of couples, no matter the species.

Hell, not even humpback whales are monogamous. Think about it. There aren't exactly humpback whale bars or sex apps. How far does a whale have to swim to get some side action?

Don't even get me started on squirrels.

They're all sluts.

So why do humans hope we're any different?

Because we wear pants (sometimes) and can talk?

My evening goes from awkward to worse when I see the only movie starting soon is a cartoon . . . featuring talking animals. The Isis is typical Aspen with its nineteenth century exterior and an updated, spare no expense interior. Of course our local theater is fancy—Aspen's Hollywood at a higher altitude where us regular folk can brush elbows with celebrities. Or brush the elbow that has brushed the famous elbow. Or something like that.

"Any chance Benedict Cumberbatch or Tom Hiddleston is voicing one of the cats?" I ask the bored woman in the ticket booth.

She catches my eye and laughs. "Sadly, no, but Chris Hemsworth is the dog next door."

Oh, I bet he is.

Ninety minutes and a bucket of fake-buttery popcorn later, I wipe the tears from my cheeks. This only manages to get salt in my already red eyes.

"Damn animal movies," I mumble to myself.

Before leaving, I duck into the bathroom to splash water on my face. Satisfied I look like I'm suffering from bad allergies and not a big cry baby who can't handle a kids' movie, I tug my hat over my hair and stroll through the empty lobby.

Once I'm outside, the cold air dispels the cozy feeling of a dark, warm theater. I pass a few couples laughing and canoodling on my way to my car. When I pass the Jerome, I notice the red carpet is gone, as is the crowd. The exterior is back to its nineteenth century simplicity.

Unable to resist, I peek inside as I walk by the glass doors. The pretty people still crowd the lobby and bar, but it looks like the party has moved on, like it always does.

I wonder if the women from before snuck in to brush against fame and power, hopeful some of the magic will rub off on them. All I can see is bright shiny teeth, flashes of expensive clothes, and bone structure that wins the genetic lottery.

"So out of my element," I mutter to myself as I skulk back to my car like a feral cat around humans.

Happily back at home, I pour myself a bath and pick up the medical periodical George defaced earlier with his kitty brown-eye.

A glass of crisp white wine, my favorite Ed Sheeran playlist cued up on Spotify, and a bath bomb should be the cure to the ordinary blues.

For a minute or two I miss Geoffrey.

Then I remember how boring our life together would be.

I'm not average.

I don't want normal.

Jesse with Fern on his shoulders skiing down a mountain enters my head for the thousandth time.

Strong, manly Jesse with his fearless job saving people.

No, I don't want boring and typical.

My mind wanders to Landon, the Viking with an edge.

He's not exactly painful to look at either.

If he asked me out, I'd say yes.

I have nothing to lose.

EIGHT

MARA

THE REST OF my first official work week is uneventful. I spend my days in the clinic or helping out in the shelter office. Life carries on normally. No beer gardens and drinking in the last of the afternoon sun surrounded by beautiful people. The ski slopes and streets of Aspen feel like a fantasyland even though they're less than twenty minutes away.

I wonder if this is how people in Orlando or Anaheim feel about living down the road from the happiest places on Earth.

After work, I go to the grocery store in Snowmass. The only tell it's not a normal market are the cans of oxygen by the shopping baskets. Welcome to life at altitude.

I fill my cart with single girl staples: boneless, skinless chicken breasts; salad mix; yogurt; vanilla coffee creamer; hummus and pita chips; and last, but most important, ice cream.

In the pet aisle, I pick up treats for the beasts at home. If George had his way, the ice cream would be for him. Too bad he's lactose intolerant—you don't want to know the details.

Mentally checking off my shopping list, I turn the corner to the registers.

When I hear a familiar chuckle, I quickly duck back into

the aisle.

Jesse stands at the nearest register. My body switches into a flight instinct before I can question why. There's no reason for me to hide from him.

Other than the whole awkward forgettable sexing.

And the part about accidentally stalking him on his fancy red carpet date.

I peek around the corner like a marmot popping his head out of a woodpile. I'm lightning quick, but I get a good glimpse of him smiling at the cashier.

He's one of those naturally friendly guys. As I spy, he chats her up, laughing and flirting while thoughtfully bagging his own groceries.

Of course the cashier is putty in his hands. Doesn't matter if she's old enough to be his mother, she touches her hair and pats his arm, displaying the classic signs of interest.

No one can blame her.

He's irresistible.

Which means I need to resist him.

I wonder if there's a local support group for the women who fall for his charms and become addicted. We can bring cupcakes and cookies, sit in a circle, and share our experiences of being the center of his attention however briefly.

Makes more sense why he didn't recognize me. How can he keep track of the dozens of women he's seduced over the years?

After a friendly wave, he picks up his bag of groceries to leave. I lean against the shelving to avoid detection. My hip bumps a bag of spaghetti and it slides off the stack, creating a small waterfall of pasta.

I try to stop the falling noodles with one hand, while still gripping my basket with the other, but fail. The basket knocks over a display of marinara sauce and next thing I know, I'm standing in a crime scene.

Broken glass, pasta, and sauce pool together on the floor. Red splatters cover my jeans and boots.

I'm still holding my basket, so I consider it a small win.

And Jesse missed the need for a cleanup in aisle four. He's probably out in the parking lot by now.

Or standing at the end of the row, a confused smile on his face.

"Hey, Doc, what's up?"

"Oh, nothing. Picking up a few things for dinner." Holding up my basket, I act normal.

"Having pasta?" Amusement lights up his eyes and he pulls his bottom lip into his mouth.

"No, why do you ask?" I step away from the carnage.

"I'll let Marjorie know to send someone over to clean up. Did you see who did it?"

He's teasing me. There's no way he doesn't see the evidence staining my jeans.

"Probably mice." I manage to keep a straight face.

He sweeps his eyes down my body and stares at my shoes for a bit before lifting his gaze to my face.

"Sounds . . . plausible."

I point to his bag. "I don't want to keep you."

"No problem. I was hoping to run into you." He takes my basket out of my hands. "I have something for you."

A restraining order?

"You finished shopping?" He studies the contents of my basket. "You don't want your ice cream to melt."

"All done."

"No pasta?"

"I try to avoid gluten." It's a lie. Gluten, aka carbs, is one of my best friends.

"Good to know." He leads me over to the same register he used. "Marjorie, this is Mara. She's the new vet working at

Hawks Creek."

"And destroyer of the pasta aisle," I confess. "I'll pay for everything."

She waves away my admission of guilt. "Nice to meet you. Don't worry about it. You wouldn't believe the stuff that happens in this market."

Jesse stands beside me as she scans my groceries. His proximity makes me want to jump with every beep. I bite the inside of my bottom lip to stop myself from blurting about our first meeting. The tabloid magazines get all of my attention until I see his face staring back at me from a small photo on the cover of Celebrity Style. His wavy hair and golden eyes have been airbrushed to perfection to complement Willow's flawless beauty. Their outfits from the Aspen party. I body block the cover from his view.

Covered in splatter from the marinara massacre, I feel foolish for ever thinking we could have something between us. The only magazine I'll ever make the cover of is the Journal of Veterinary Medicine. No sexy cover pic in my future.

It's evident he's much better at playing things cool. He's probably had a ton of experience, I remind myself. If I can focus on his poor memory, I won't have to face my own missing pieces from that night.

At least I remember meeting him.

And the kissing.

"Cash or card, sweetie?" Marjorie asks.

"Huh?" I slowly blink at her.

"How are you going to pay?" The tone in her voice tells me she thinks I'm weird.

"Oh, right." I dig out my card and insert it into the chip reader.

She hands me my receipt. "Good luck."

With the new job? Here? With Jesse? In life?

I wish she were more specific.

The man in question sweeps my bags into his arm along with his own. "Come on, it's in my rig."

"What is?"

"Your surprise." He points down the row of cars to a gray Land Cruiser.

"You didn't have to get me anything."

"I know, but I wanted to. Think of it as a welcome to town present."

What does a guy give a girl who he thinks he just met but has seen naked already?

Even my mother would be stumped on the protocol for such a gift.

Setting down our groceries, he reaches into the backseat and then pulls out a bag. "Here you go."

Whatever is in the bag, he's excited about it. His smile is irresistible and I grin back at him.

"Thank you!" My enthusiasm might be premature given I haven't looked inside the bag yet.

"Open it," he whispers.

I'm lost for a moment in the sound of his deep voice and warm eyes.

"Go on." He touches my hand, the one holding the bag. "It won't bite."

I peek inside and see a big bow. Beneath it is a helmet.

Laughter and embarrassment create an awkward giggle-sigh in my throat. "Um, thanks?"

"For next time you're on the mountain. Red like your beanie. You can probably glue a big white fluff-ball on the top if you want."

"It's . . . lovely." And very bright red.

"Top of the line. Only the best."

I have no idea how expensive ski helmets can be until I lift it out of the bag and see the price sticker. It's more than a nice meal and almost a car payment.

"You really shouldn't have. I'm thinking of sticking to the lodge at base village for the rest of the season."

He looks like I punched him. "Why?"

Because I'm a scaredy cat homebody who prefers hot cocoa to double-black anxiety attacks? Because I'm trying to avoid him and after today will probably drive down valley to shop for food in bulk? I'm sure a case of boxed mac n' cheese will last me for months. My freezer can probably hold at least two weeks of Lean Cuisines. Cereal is a great meal no matter the time of day.

Why does he have to be nice and buy me presents?

Doesn't he feel the awkward?

Oh right. He doesn't.

Because I'm a stranger to him.

I place the helmet, with bow still attached, on my head to demonstrate my gratitude. "It's perfect. I can wear it cross-country skiing. Or snowshoeing. Do people wear helmets when they ice skate? They should. Ice is dangerous."

He's still frowning. "You didn't answer my question about skiing."

Not out loud at least. I stare at my feet. Wearing my helmet in a parking lot, I try to think of something clever to say.

"Hey." He ducks down into my field of vision. "Too soon?"

"No, it's a really thoughtful gift. You shouldn't have spent the money." How much can ski patrollers make? "It's too much."

"I have an idea. I have a weekend day off. We'll go back up the mountain and I'll give you some lessons. You have all the basics. You just need more confidence."

"Lessons?"

He knocks on my helmet. "Yes, I'm volunteering. Or I can sign you up for lessons with Tegian the Norwegian."

"The who-what?"

"You are new around here. Everyone knows Tegian. He's a legend on the slopes. I think he was on the Norwegian Olympic team in the eighties. Or maybe it was the seventies."

"How old is he?"

"Old enough. He still skies in a one-piece rainbow jumpsuit sometimes."

I imagine an older guy with a major moose knuckle swooshing down the slopes. I'm not sure I've had worse ideas than trying to picture Tegian in all his glory.

"Hot, right? He's hard to compete with. All the ladies love the Norwegian."

"I choose you." The words fly out of my mouth before I can stop them. I don't even want to take lessons.

Maybe if we spend more time together, he'll remember me. Or I'll work up the nerve to tell him.

I should tell him now. Rip off the Band-Aid. Lose the cone of shame.

"You know, we've—"

His phone rings and he glances at the screen. "Hold that thought."

I swallow my confession and bury it back inside my chest.

"Hi, Willow. Sure. No, I'm not doing anything. Just at the store." He smiles at me before taking a few steps away for privacy. When he reaches the hood, he leans against it, leaving me standing by myself, wearing a helmet in a parking lot.

Willow from the fancy party. Willow Cross who has it all goin' on. He hasn't mentioned seeing me in Aspen, so maybe, for once, I flew under his radar.

I'm tempted to test out my helmet by banging my head on the side of his car, but I'm worried about causing damage. To the car.

Before I can test out my resilience, he's back. "Sorry about that. An old friend is in town for a few days. You know how it is when you haven't seen someone in a long time."

Oh boy. "Sure. Of course."

Old friend doesn't sound like a passionate love. Then again, he's not going to tell a practical stranger about his famous girlfriend.

He continues talking. "I'm off on Sundays. Give me your number and I'll text you. We can meet at base village. I think we'll avoid Sam's Knob this time and try out Elk Camp. How do you feel about gondolas?"

"They're romantic?"

He lifts an eyebrow.

"Venice. Gondolas." I remove my helmet.

"I meant on the mountain."

"Right." Of course. I should stop talking. When I'm around him, my lizard brain takes over and I'm no longer able to process big words or complex concepts. Or focus. Obviously.

"Give me your phone." He wiggles his fingers. I dig my phone out of my bag and unlock it before handing it to him. He punches in his number and sends himself a text. "All set."

"Alrighty then. Thanks for this." I swing the helmet in case he forgot. "I'll see you around I guess."

"You're welcome." His smile is addicting. All straight, white teeth and those gorgeous soft lips.

"See you." I walk backward a few steps before turning and heading to my own car. When I reach the end of the row I realize I've walked in the opposite direction from where I parked and I'll have to pass him again when I retrace my steps.

He's leaning against his bumper when I loop back around. In his hand is my grocery bag.

"Forget something?" He holds up the tote.

"I was distracted by my awesome helmet." Faking an "aren't I ridiculous" smile on my face, I practically snatch the bag from his hands.

"Can you find your way home?"

I ignore his chuckle. "I think I'll manage."

"Wouldn't want you to get lost."

"There are two roads in and out of town. I'll be fine."

"Just making sure." He tips his head. For a few seconds it seems like he wants to say something more, but he doesn't.

We stand there awkwardly for another minute.

"Well, I'll be having ice cream soup for dinner. Enjoy your evening!" I wave with the arm holding my bag and it knocks into my hip.

His expression tells me he's worried I might maim myself.

Forcing myself not to rush, I casually walk to my little blue Honda CRV.

Smooth.

How am I going to survive an entire day of ski lessons with him?

On the drive home I contemplate faking a sprained ankle with an ace bandage.

NINE

MARA

ON MONDAY, I attend a board meeting for the ranch. The only person I recognize besides Elizabeth is Sage. She's a little younger than I am, but apparently comes from a wealthy family in Chicago. Because of her, I have a job. Besides being responsible for me having a job here, she's also a nice person. I can see us hanging out, if I ever get the nerve up to ask her to coffee or whatever the mountain equivalent is.

Elizabeth calls the meeting to order. Along with me and Sage, three other women sit around the long conference table. Mary is the volunteer representative. She's wearing a red and black plaid shirt covered in Scottie dogs. I'm introduced to everyone else and I give a short speech about my background and goals for the new clinic.

Sage smiles at me encouragingly when I finish.

Elizabeth introduces the agenda and I notice the first item concerns sled dogs. There's been a lot of controversy in recent years about kennels and treatment of these working dogs. I wasn't aware of any local sledding operations.

"We want to partner with Mushers Kennel in Aspen to make sure the dogs are fairly treated. Additionally, it's important to avoid a PR disaster if there are any issues. We don't need protests and animal rights boycotts in town."

"The dogs should come first before any tourism concerns," I speak up after she finishes her statement.

"Of course. We don't have any existing concerns. Mushers has always done their best to be fair to the dogs, but they're working animals, not pets."

"Ski patrol has working dogs. They live with their humans and are members of the family. Why can't the same be done with the sled dogs?" Sage offers.

I think of Jesse skiing down the mountain with Fern on his shoulders. "The bonding helps train the dogs. I'm not sure if the same is true for mushers."

"Let's reach out to them and see how we can work together. Mara, it's important for you to introduce yourself. Make sure they know we're here for any medical needs."

I make a note to research other sled dog kennels to determine acceptable protocols.

Elizabeth moves on to the next item. "We were contacted about a potential animal hoarder outside Glenwood. There could be a dozen dogs and over twenty cats. Animal control will be visiting the property this week. Typically in these cases, the pets are neglected and will need medical care. Mara and I will be on standby to drive to Glenwood with the van if their shelters can't handle the influx."

The rest of the meeting is about volunteer schedules and fundraising. My limited staff of vet techs falls under Sage's funding, but I feel obligated to give input on ideas to bring in more donations. For every dog or cat, goat or horse, we rescue, there are hundreds still in need of help. If I think of how many animals are neglected or abused, I would spend my days in tears. I need to focus on the things we can do, not be overwhelmed by the magnitude of the need.

Mushers could be the perfect chance to make a difference and be part of a larger impact.

Tuesdays are spay and neuter day at the clinic.

I like to blast music while I operate. It helps break up the monotony of the repetitive procedures. Some surgeons like classic music. I don't do pretentious. I like old school hip-hop and often sing along.

Yeah, I know all the words to "Rappers' Delight."

If I were the kind of girl who sings karaoke, I'd kill it with that song. Mic drop.

However, for me, singing in front of people is up there with public nudity and back hair on humans on a list of things I'd like to avoid.

Dying alone and having cats nibble away my toes tops the list.

This is where my brain goes.

Being single isn't the worst thing in the world.

Or so the women's magazines tell me right after the articles about trends in pubic hair and how to please my man six ways to Saturday before I spend Sunday baking cupcakes from scratch.

I swear I only read those magazines in waiting rooms. Or on planes. Or in line at the grocery store.

Our small lobby here at the ranch needs more trashy magazines. All we have are *Horse and Hound*, *Dog Fancy*, *Cat Fancy*, and the super trendy, *Goat Fancy*.

Pygmy goats are this decade's pot-bellied mini pig.

You can put pajamas on a goat, but that doesn't make them a house pet.

The clinic has two vet techs on staff along with me. Before Sage gave her endowment, Elizabeth made due with volunteers and agreements with local vets down valley to handle all the shelter's needs.

Now that I'm here and I have a small staff, we do everything in-house, as well as provide free spay and neutering once a month to local pet owners.

My techs, Teresa and Beth, are pros at neutering.

Like most things in life, anything having to do with females is more complicated.

Castration? Give me five minutes and I've got it covered.

Probably not something I should ever mention on a date.

This may be another reason I'm single. I'm perfectly fine with removing balls.

Today we snip and sew ten male cats, and spay five females along with a couple of dogs who were transported to us from the hoarder house.

After everyone is coned and comfortable in recovery, we clean up the surgery room.

"Mara," Lisa, our receptionist, calls me over the intercom.

I press speak with my elbow. "Yes?"

"You have a visitor up front."

"I'm not expecting anyone." I finish drying my hands on a paper towel and then toss it in the trash.

"He says he'll wait."

He?

The only "he" I know is Jesse.

Or Lee Barnard, but wouldn't she say it was Lee given he's Sage's boyfriend and has a goat barn named after him?

I walk out of the surgical room and down the hall trying to prepare myself for disappointment if it's not Jesse.

Landon stands at the reception desk, laughing with Lisa. He leans on the counter and smiles at something on her computer. Their heads are practically touching.

"Uh, hi?" I interrupt them.

Landon's eyes sweep over to me, then slowly trail down my

body from my shoulders to my legs. Not sure if he has a thing for scrubs, but I don't think he can see anything of interest unless he's attracted to cats in outer space.

Yes, they're as awesome as they sound.

"Nice outfit."

"Thanks. No one in space can hear you meow." I laugh at my own joke.

Landon doesn't.

Lisa takes a couple extra beats before she giggles.

Landon still doesn't laugh.

Okay, so sci-fi horror humor with cats isn't his jam.

He clears his throat. "I wanted to talk to you about something."

Lisa picks up several folders from the desk and mentions needing to file them. I'm pretty sure the ones in her hands are all empty, but I don't argue with her.

"Can I help you with something animal related? Do you want to adopt a pet?"

He makes a face at the mention of a pet.

Whoa.

"No pets?" I ask.

"No time for the extra responsibility."

A warning siren like the kind used for tornadoes begins to sound in the distance, but I'm the only one who can hear it.

"Life can keep us busy." I tilt my head to the side as I wonder what he's doing at the shelter if he doesn't have a pet nor does he seem interested in obtaining one.

"I decided we should go out to dinner. You're new here and probably don't know anyone. I imagine you're lonely. So I'm here to ask you out. There's an incredible and authentic creperie in Aspen." He does a strange accent for creperie that might be French or his best Celine Dion impression. Hard to tell.

My head tilts to the opposite side like a dog when she hears an odd sound. "Are you asking me out on a date?"

Why can I be straightforward with Landon and not with Jesse?

Maybe because Landon's cool Viking smugness doesn't turn me on. I feel about as hot as a fjord in the winter.

Still, he did mention crepes.

While his invite is vaguely, to put it lightly, insulting, he's also right. I don't really know anyone in town. I spend most evenings playing referee between Tapper and George. Fred acts like he doesn't know either of them, which is no help at all.

"Okay. I like crepes." Honestly, my enthusiasm for an evening with Landon is directly proportional to my love of crepes.

"Great. We can meet there. Are you free Friday night? What am I saying, you probably are."

My jaw drops and my mouth opens.

Crepes, think of the crepes.

He could be awkward because of nerves. He had smoother lines during après ski.

I hesitate for a few seconds. "Friday works."

"Great. We'll meet at seven." He stares over my shoulder.

I love crepes.

"Sure. See you then." I give him a small wave, then drop my hand.

He flashes me a smug smile and saunters out the front door.

Crepes, crepes, crepes, crepes.

Lisa returns and sets the same folders on the desk. "You can buy your own crepes, you know."

Her admission of eavesdropping makes me laugh. "I'm trying to be open minded and say yes to new things."

She narrows her eyes at me. "Suit yourself."

Her flat tone isn't exactly a vote of confidence.

TEN

MARA

I HAVE A date.

I think it's a date and not a welcome to town dinner.

Landon didn't say it was a date. Neither did he mention anyone else joining us.

He's also not picking me up. Ride giving implies a date.

Still, I need to prepare.

He clearly doesn't understand the awesomeness of cats in space. I'll need an outfit that says mature and sexy.

Easy. Because of course I have a closet full of those kinds of clothes.

I open the doors and stare into the sea of jeans, boring black work pants, scrubs in animal patterns, responsible shirts, basic sweaters, and T-shirts I've owned since college. In the back of the closet are a few sundresses and a black dress more appropriate for funerals than a date.

When does my fairy godmother arrive to turn this all into something fabulous?

In the past, if I needed a special outfit, I'd raid Sofie's closet. She owns things with sequins and fringe. I own non-wrinkle black pants and clogs.

I text her an SOS.

My phone rings and I jump.

No one but my mother ever actually uses the phone to make calls.

I'm relieved to see Sofie's name on the screen.

"Why are you calling me?"

"You texted me."

"Which means I expected a text in return. Not using our real voices." I lower mine and add a terrible French accent, "Vhat if zey are lissening to us?"

"Who? No one cares what we talk about." She's not laughing. Not even a giggle.

"You're no fun at all."

"Then why are you calling me?"

"I need to raid your closet."

"You're kind of far away to raid my closet in Boston." She's silent for a few beats. "Why?"

"I have a date," I whisper.

"Should I ask why you're whispering? Is he there already?"

"No, I don't want the cats to find out. You know how jealous they get if they think they're going to have to share my attention with someone else."

"What about the dog?" I hear rustling on her end of the call.

"They barely acknowledge his existence. It's the best way to maintain peace."

"You're really weird." True, but I amuse her.

"Old news. Moving on. I need an outfit for a dinner date."

"With?"

"A man." I give her nothing.

"I hate you."

"I'm not sure if I like him or not." I don't say anything about the Norse god hotness or charms of a serial killer. I don't want her to worry.

"Then why are you going out on a date with him?"

"He invited me to the crepe place in Aspen."

"You love crepes." I hear the thunk of something heavy hitting a carpeted floor. "Okay, I get it now."

"What are you doing?" I ask.

"You don't want to know."

"Plausible deniability?"

"Better that way. You should wear jeans and your black lace top with the high neck. The outfit needs to say 'I like sex, but I'm not sure if I'm going to have it with you' in a classy way."

"All that from a top and jeans?"

"You'd be surprised. The lace will make him think of lingerie. The high neck says Victorian lady."

She has a good point. "Thanks. Please don't go to jail. I'm not sure what I'd do without you."

"Orange has never been my color. And if I'm in jail, how will I come out and visit you in a few months?"

I miss her. There's nothing like a best friend who will always have your back.

Feeling better after our call, I get ready for the evening.

I'm not exactly optimistic I've met my soul mate in Landon, but I'm not dreading dinner.

Will this dinner ever end?

How long can a man talk without taking a breath or pausing to sip some water? How is it possible his throat isn't parched?

I smile and reach for my glass. Torn between my desire to do something to stave off a yawn and adding more liquid to my bladder, I toy with the stem. Instead of drinking, I flip my knife back and forth next to my plate like I'm flipping a coin.

Blade facing in. Pee my pants before he stops talking.

Blade facing out. Run screaming for the bathroom.

Blade in. Blade out. It's the world's worst, least dangerous knife game.

I've had to pee since we sat down, but there hasn't been a break in his monologue long enough for me to politely excuse myself to the ladies' room.

At least now he's moved on from talk of his passion for water sports.

The typical kind.

I hope.

My poor bladder.

I squirm and recross my legs while I wait for the right moment to escape.

Landon must take my wiggling as excitement because he smiles at me and says, "Right?"

"Sure." I have no clue what he's said and pray I haven't just agreed to something horrible, like a big game hunt or a second date.

I wonder if this is what racehorses feel like. Where does the expression "pee like a racehorse" come from anyway? Does a full bladder make them run faster? Or is it all horses? Do the other equines tease the racehorses about holding it so long? As a veterinarian, I feel like I should know the answer to these questions, but as a small animal vet, it's out of my repertoire.

I need to stop thinking about peeing. I should focus on dry things.

Like California's drought, month old Christmas trees, British wit. And my vagina while listening to the world's most boring date mansplain to me about his fantasy football club.

Zoning out on his pretend football team's stats, I plant a vague, but interested smile on my face and stare over his shoulder. Behind him, a waiter fills glasses of water for the table of four chic women. To their left, a waitress opens a bottle of wine and pours a few splashes into the bowl of a large goblet.

A couple on the right sips a creamy soup from large spoons. When a toddler in a high chair tips over his mom's glass of water and the liquid creates a waterfall from the table to the floor, I reach my breaking point.

"Hold that thought!" I practically leap from my chair and speed toward the bathroom, keeping my hand pressed against my abdomen to encourage my pelvis muscles to not give up the fight just yet.

I plow past the woman leaving the single occupancy bathroom with a quick thank you as she momentarily fights to maintain her hold on the door. With a quick tug, the door shuts and I fumble with the lock while my other hand begins undoing my jeans.

"Ahhhh," I moan with relief. If someone were eavesdropping, they might think I'm in here having sex with how loud I am.

Finishing up and washing my hands at the sink, I frown at myself in the mirror. One month in Colorado and I've broken my biggest rule.

No more boring dates with boring men who don't realize how boring they are.

Life's too short.

On paper, Landon seems . . . nice.

I'm not going to lie and say his name didn't have something to do with me accepting the date. Landon, like Michael Landon. Pa on Little House on the Prairie was my first great crush. I know, I probably should've crushed on Almanzo, but Pa was so manly and kind. Not every man can pull off suspenders and make it hot. Don't get me started about all his thick, wavy brown hair and his broad shoulders. There's something about a man who can build things with his hands. Throw in the fiddle playing and the gentle strength, how could anyone resist?

This Landon is proving more than easy to resist.

At least both men share the manly part. Or at least I assume it's a penis Landon keeps touching beneath the tablecloth.

I dry my hands on a paper towel from the neat stack in a basket next to the sink.

If I'm being honest, I also said yes to the date to check out this restaurant. La Belle Femme is charming in a shabby but elegant way only the French can ever pull off. Their crepes are to die for.

Or at least worth putting up with a boring date and a nearly burst bladder.

Winding my way through the intimate restaurant crowded with small tables, I witness two things almost simultaneously.

First, Landon is chatting up our waitress like they're old friends. Or old friends with benefits. His hand is on her slim waist, and as I spy on them, he moves it lower to give her a pinch. On her ass. While me, his lovely date, is in the bathroom.

Second, standing at the hostess desk is Jesse. He's grinning at the slim hostess like he wants to roll her up in a crepe and have her for dessert.

If I had my bag with me, I'd keep walking straight out the door without a backward glance.

What is it with guys in this town? Do they think they're the only men in the world? Has the altitude addled their brains into thinking they're gods among us mere female mortals? Blessing us with their presence and attention one minute, taking it away the next because something else has caught their fancy? Because they can?

The waitress laughs a little too loud, drawing not only my attention but Jesse's.

As his gaze sweeps the room, his eyes land on me.

Great.

Now he's seen my date flirting with the waitress.

I don't care about Landon and his imaginary sports team,

but I do care about the humiliation of being *that* girl. The one whose date is a loser. A cad. A bad stereotype.

I can do better.

Ignoring Jesse, I breeze through the tables to Landon while forming my excuse.

Once I reach him, I gently place my hand on his forearm, inches away from where he's fondling another woman's hip.

"Sorry to interrupt, but I need to go. Emergency at the clinic." My words might be polite, but my tone says I'm through. Or something that rhymes with through but sounds more like "fuck you."

Our waitress jumps a few inches to the side. Her long blond-highlighted hair swings behind her back like Rapunzel. Landon's hand hovers in the air like he's falling off a cliff and she's the rope he'd been clinging to.

"You're a doctor?" Pretty waitress blinks her warm brown eyes at me.

"She's only a vet." Landon corrects her.

"Right." My voice is as cold and flat as a metal pole. "Well—" I'm about to say thank you for a lovely evening because being polite is so ingrained into me, but I stop myself. With a quick nod, I turn and walk away.

Really, what more needed to be said?

"Only a vet," I mumble as I collect my coat from the rack next to the front door. "Only a vet coming from a guy who probably got his associates degree online. Just a vet."

I'm so infuriated by his insult I can't get my arm in the sleeve of my coat. Wrestling with the puffy tube of death, I spin myself around like a dog trying to catch its own tail.

"Only a—"

A hand stops my spinning. "Here, let me help."

I recognize Jesse's deep voice. My knight in a down parka holds onto the sleeve of my coat.

"I don't need rescuing," I say without an effort to sound grateful.

"If you'd like to continue your whirling dervish impression, by all means, don't let me get in your way." He drops my coat and steps away.

I grudgingly shove my arm into the sleeve and tug my parka over my shoulder.

"This is the part where you say thank you," he suggests quietly.

Under normal circumstances, I would—because it's the polite thing to do—but I'm riled up and don't want to do the expected.

"I didn't need your help."

"Never said you did." He stares over my shoulder. "You're on a date?"

"More of a social experiment." I refuse to turn around.

"He doesn't look very happy."

"Good." I'm being petulant, but ask me if I care.

"Was he a jerk to you?" Jesse straightens his back and rolls his shoulders, making him appear more like a bear than a man.

"To me, to the waitress, although she didn't seem to mind."

Jesse's eyes flash to mine. "Seriously? He flirted with the waitress in front of you?"

"No, he did the gentlemanly thing and waited until I was in the bathroom."

He stares down at me and his lips part like he's about to say something but is trying to resist. With a shake of his head, he erases the words. Instead, he runs his fingers across the center of his forehead. "Right."

I don't know what he means. Is he agreeing with my sarcastic remark about Landon's manners? As I'm trying to figure out his strange response, he gives a smug look behind me.

"Wha—"

I don't finish the word. Or the thought. Because Jesse kisses me. Right in the middle of La Belle Femme. Blocking the front door. In front of the entire restaurant.

It's not a peck on the lips. *Oh no.*

He wraps an arm around me, pressing his forearm into my back and shifts us so he can properly kiss me. His tongue invades my mouth and it's not at all polite or mannered. No. This is the kind of kissing that puts the tongue in PDA. Not the sort of kissing you do in public. Not even in a romantic French restaurant. This is a kiss I feel spark throughout my body, igniting dormant, parched areas and setting them aflame.

My body remembers this kiss. We're still kissing soul mates.

I press my hand against his shoulder, unsure if I mean to push him away or pull him closer, but my touch snaps him out of the kiss. He leans away, settling me back on my feet, and brushing his hand over my shoulders.

My feelings are a jumbled mess inside my head. Should I feel thankful? Insulted? Turned on? Assaulted? All of the above? *What the hell just happened?*

His big hands gently lift my hair out of my coat and set it free. He tugs on a curl and lets it bounce back into shape before speaking. "There. All better."

The gesture is both sweet and confusing.

I couldn't be more confused if he sprouted fur and actually turned into a bear right in front of my eyes. Why am I always thinking about bears when he's around?

"Uh, what was that?" I whisper, casting a glance to see if everyone is staring at us. My focus wanders over to the table I'd occupied with Landon a few minutes ago. It's empty.

"Sorry to interrupt," the hostess speaks up, "but your friend left without paying."

Simultaneously, like synchronized swimmers, Jesse and I turn to face her.

"Sorry." She holds up the bill folder. "He said you'd take care of it."

"When did he leave?" I whisper.

"While you two were kissing. He stomped out of here. You didn't see him?"

My eyes widen. How long were we kissing that my date up and left, sticking me with the tab? What sort of voodoo magic did Jesse wield over me?

"It happened really fast," our waitress joins the conversation. "Jesse helped you with your coat and by the time you two were lip locked, Landon was on his way out the door."

"Hi, Mae." Jesse gives her a little wave and an embarrassed half-smile.

"Hey, Jesse." She waves.

"You two know each other?" I ask, my focus split between the two of them.

"Forever," they both reply at the same time.

"It's a small town," Mae says.

"Especially if you grew up here," Jesse adds.

"Sorry about your date." Mae gives me an empathetic smile. "I've known Landon a long time. You dodged a bullet there. Thanks to Jesse."

"Oh, the date was DOA before he showed up." I don't bother sharing the "just a vet" comment. Moot point.

"I didn't really get the date vibe from your table. Then when you went to the bathroom, he started chatting me up."

Feeling you up is more like it.

"He's always been a handsy guy. Knows we won't make a big fuss because the customer's always right and we work for tips. I should've stayed on the other side of the table." She's pretty in a pierced-nose, carefree, naturally pretty kind of way.

"Please don't apologize for his actions. He's a jerk," I say.

"You were on a real date with Landon?" Jesse interrupts.

"There won't be a second one."

"Why was there a first one? Of all the men in town, you thought to yourself, Landon Roberts is the one for me?" He shakes his head in disgust, or maybe disbelief.

"It was just a date. I love crepes."

"Then come for crepes by yourself."

While I agree with him on almost everything he's said, I'm not going to admit it. What business is it of his?

"And be the lonely woman dining all alone?"

"I'm here. You could've come with me."

I stare at him.

"As friends. This town's too small to date locals. Right, Mae?"

Mae glances between us and holds up her hands. "No comment."

Wait a hot minute. Does that mean she and Jesse have already dated? If they've known each other forever, the odds are likely they have. I can see them together with their Colorado fresh-faces and excellent genes swooshing down mountains while laughing and being good looking.

Who hasn't he dated?

Other than me.

And probably the table of ladies with the giant rocks on their hands and Botox in their faces.

"Thanks for the tip."

"No problem." He picks up a to-go bag from the hostess stand. "It's been fun, ladies."

He gives me a slight nod and leaves, cold air blowing in behind him when he opens the door.

"Wow," Mae says. "I've never seen him do that before."

"Kiss a random woman in public?"

She shifts her gaze to her desk, avoiding the truth we all know. "Not that part."

"Didn't think so." He'd kissed me within a minute of

meeting me for the first time.

"Defend a woman's honor. That's what I was going to say." She wraps her long hair around in a loose bun at the nape of her neck.

"Is that what he did? Whose honor?"

"I meant yours. He doesn't like when the customers get flirty, but we all know it's part of the business."

"Mine?"

"He watched the whole thing go down at the table."

"Wonderful. Nothing like creating a scene."

"Oh, don't worry about that. It's so dark in here, I doubt anyone could see past their own noses." She smiles and it's genuinely friendly. "How do you know Jesse?"

"I don't really. We've . . ." I pause to think of how to phrase it so I wasn't giving away the whole sordid past, " . . . met a few times. He rescued me from a panic attack on the mountain a few weeks ago."

"I see. You didn't ask for my thoughts, but I'll tell you I've known him for over a decade. Super nice guy. Terrible boyfriend material."

Her words ring true, but the truth doesn't stop the disappointment from taking up residence in my chest.

"I get the feeling you're new to town."

"Is it obvious?"

She laughed. "You'll see how it is. Might be a glamorous ski destination, but it's still a small town. If you're looking for friends, some of us get together and go to Taco Tuesdays. It's a girls only night and I think you'd fit right in with the group."

"I'd love to join."

Mae and I exchange numbers and then I reach for my wallet.

She waves away my credit card. "Your bill's been taken care of."

"I thought you said my date left it for me."

"He did. Jesse paid for it." She flashes me a grin.

That man! I didn't know if I wanted to yell at him or kiss him again.

ELEVEN

JESSE

LANDON ROBERTS?

OF all the guys in town, Mara goes to dinner with him?

I can't believe anyone would go out with that hooker clown.

Apologies to all clowns and rugby players.

He puts the prick in the PRC: Pitkin Rugby Club.

He doesn't just play a hooker on the pitch.

I stop short on the sidewalk at the thought of Mara fucking a guy like Landon.

Sometimes, okay, majority of the time, I don't understand women.

How many times do you see a beautiful, smart, funny, interesting woman with a scumbag? Too many to count. Sure, sometimes money or power trumps a personality disorder, but the statistics are too high to ignore.

I'm a nice guy. We've established this.

I save people for a living. How much nicer can a guy get? I'm nice when I'm not being paid. Hell, I bought her a helmet. I have a dog.

Landon showing up at the beer garden surprised me, and yet it didn't. He can sniff out fresh blood like a Great White.

The man has the same dead eyes and cold heart of a shark. Yet Mara goes to dinner with Landon. Maybe he's her type.

If that's the case, explains why she acts like we've never met before. The details of that night came back to me when we ran into each other at the market. Her rambling charm is one of a kind. How could I ever forget her kiss?

Back at the restaurant, I decided to kiss her to see if it would help her remember.

Isn't this how kisses always work in fairy tales?

Hell if I cared we had an audience. The same chemistry I felt two years ago is still there. After hesitating, she kissed me back, full tilt.

Yet she still acts like she doesn't remember me.

I could be dodging a major crazy woman bullet.

Hiding my take-out bag behind me, I step up to the counter to pay for my movie ticket.

"I know you're bringing in contraband food, Jesse." Thea stares at me when she hands me my change. "You know we sell food at the snack bar."

I give her a grin. "Yes, but you don't have Nutella and banana crepes, do you?"

"No, we have popcorn and Raisinets like a typical movie theater."

"I wanted dessert."

"At least this time you're not bringing in an entire large pizza."

"Everyone loved me." It's been a long standing tradition for me to bring my own snacks to the movies going back over twenty years. I don't like popcorn.

"Next time bring some to share." She peers over her glasses at me like she used to do when she worked as the receptionist up at the middle school.

I'm still smiling as I take my usual spot in the middle, two rows from the back of the small theater. The lights dim as I settle into my seat, unwrapping my crepe.

It's still warm and the chocolate drips over the side. I suck a spot on the side of my hand. Forget fancy dinner with candlelight, crepes are street food meant to be eaten without a fork or knife.

The trailers are still playing when the door to the lobby opens and a woman walks in, her hat familiar as she takes a seat directly in front of me.

Going to see an action movie after a bad date wouldn't be my first choice, but I'm not a girl. I'm surprised I'm happy to see her. Maybe I'm the crazy one.

Mara takes off her coat and hat, then reclines her seat. I spy a bag of popcorn tucked next to her on the chair and hold back a gag.

Without thinking, I lean forward so I'm close to her head and whisper, "You can do better."

She startles, but doesn't punch me. Thankfully. Her shriek echoes around the theater as the sound quiets between trailers.

"Jesus, you scared me!" She twists in her seat to face me.

"It's Jesse. I can see how you can get the names confused." I pick up my stuff and move to sit next to her.

"What are you eating?" She points at the mess of chocolate in my hand.

"Nutella and banana crepe." I take a bite.

"At the movies? You're weird." She eats a handful of disgusting popcorn.

"Don't knock it until you try it. I'm guessing your date imploded before you had time to order dessert."

She ducks her head away from me. "I can't believe you witnessed everything. I'm now a spectacle for town gossip. On a date with one guy and kissing another at the hostess stand."

"Hey, look at me." I wait for her to turn to face me again.

"You're not a spectacle. People do crazy stuff around here all the time. Anyone who's lived here long enough knows Landon and his reputation. If anything, people might feel sorry he duped you into thinking he's a nice guy."

"When I first met him, I thought he could fit the profile of a serial killer."

I bark out a short laugh and get shushed by an older couple closer to the front. The movie hasn't even started yet.

"You thought he might murder you and you still went to dinner with him?"

Mystery solved. She has terrible taste in men. My theory about nice women dating assholes is proven right. Feeling self-satisfied, I finish off the crepe in two bites.

There's no way I'm admitting we made out a couple of years ago. It's not worth the drama or awkwardness if she's into hooker wannabe bad boys.

"I'm trying to be more open and adventurous. I told myself I'm going to say yes to everything, within reason. And I really like crepes."

"Including eating French food with a potential killer?"

"I wouldn't have gone if I really thought he was a psychopath. Or even a sociopath."

The movie begins and we're forced to halt our conversation. I'm not even paying attention to the plot set up because I'm too busy stewing over her admission about Landon.

The question is no longer *if* she's crazy.

It's about how crazy she is.

She munches away on her popcorn, oblivious to my annoyance.

I can't figure her out.

She's a vet, so she's obviously smart and driven.

She moved to a new state and small town by herself, so she has some self-confidence and a sense of adventure.

I stare at her out of the corner of my eye. She's put effort into her appearance tonight. Her curls are tamed and smooth. Gloss or lipstick darkens her lips, but not in an over the top way. In the dark I can't pick out the color of her eyes, but from memory I know they're a deep blue like a high alpine lake. Underneath her coat, her curves fill out her jeans and the black top I spotted at the restaurant. She's beautiful in a natural way. I catch a whiff of vanilla and fresh raspberries that is all her. I lean closer as a heaviness settles in my cock. I'm not insta-hard, but certain parts of my body definitely remember the feel of her touch.

She clears her throat, and I realize I've been caught staring.

She leans close until we're a few inches apart and whispers, "What did you mean I can do better?"

When I said the words earlier, I meant with the popcorn as a movie snack, but now I mean in her decision making and taste in men.

"You can do better." I keep it simple.

This time our fellow movie-goer turns around and glares at us. I glower back because it's an action movie and a string of explosions fills the screen. There's no dialogue being missed by our quiet conversation, no key plot twist about why the cars go fast and sometimes crash.

Instead of enjoying senseless violence on the screen, my mind wanders back to the first night I met Mara.

My movie buzz is ruined. I shift uncomfortably as I try to deal with my body's reaction to being close to her. I kissed her tonight and flipped a switch inside of me.

Whether or not she remembers our crazy night together, I still want to get to know her.

If she's going to be dating anyone local, fuck Landon.

She should be with me.

TWELVE

JESSE

PICKING SOMEONE UP in a bar is as easy as falling down on skis. If you strap on skis, at some point you're going to fall. If you go out during ski season, hooking up with someone is inevitable.

A glance, a stare, maybe a tilt of the head, and a smile.

It's a mating game as old as time. I bet those biblical guys used the same tricks. Loose robes and sandals weren't doing any of them favors.

For all my years playing the game, I've never had a woman fall into my arms.

Until tonight.

Rescuing people is part of my job description.

It's also a stated goal for me to enhance guest experiences and initiate contact. My interpretation of my work guidelines extends off the slopes. I'm an ambassador for the ski company.

Jesse Hayes, at your service.

The night started typical enough. The guys and I stopped by Annie's to watch the playoff game while splitting a pitcher and wings. Filled with mostly locals, Annie's is always the warm up before the main action over on Hyman Avenue.

Tonight, Easley suggests we start at the Onion because it's still early. Known for their Jell-O shots, the Onion also encourages female patrons to dance on the bar. I'm sure the two have something to do with each other.

The place is packed when we arrive and the line out the door means they're already at capacity.

"I'm not waiting in line." I stop a few feet from the door.

"Who waits in line?" Easley barrels through the crowd. "We're locals."

I stand back while he chats up Chad, the bouncer. He plays rugby on the same semi-pro team as me and a bunch of the other guys I hang around.

Easley pats Chad's shoulder before giving me a "told you so" grin.

"Thanks, Chad," I say as I pass him.

"No problem. Always room for two more assholes."

I'm sure he means it as a compliment.

Inside, the crowd cheers for a group of women dancing on the bar. It's not even ten o'clock, but the games have already begun. In the mountains, people start partying at après ski and crash early to hit the fresh powder in the morning.

A group of women dance and laugh on the bar, singing along to a Katy Perry song. Their antics and moves remind me of a float in a Mardi Gras parade. The only things missing are beads. A blonde in the middle bends at the waist and flashes a lot of boob at the cheering guys watching the show. If there were beads, she'd have earned a lot of them with her move.

Just another Wednesday night in Aspen during ski season.

I squeeze through the crowd, hoping people are distracted enough I can get a drink from the bartender without waiting so long I dehydrate.

I'm about five feet from the bar when the blonde with wild curls gives a loud whoop and stage dives into the crowd. On instinct I raise my arms to prevent her from face planting. I catch her and hold on to her squirming body as she wiggles and laughs above my head.

"Easy there," I grunt out the words as I try to keep my balance before she sends us both sprawling backward. In this crowd, it would be like a domino effect if we tilt over. We could easily take out at least twenty people.

I manage to shift her weight and slide her down my front. Before I can set her on solid ground, she wraps her legs around my hips and kisses me.

Not a peck with closed lips.

She's sliding her tongue in my mouth with everything she's got.

Normally, this would be weird.

But she's an amazing kisser, so I go with it.

The crowd around us yells about getting a room and I'm sure there's going to be a video of this posted on social media somewhere within minutes.

She releases her legs and dangles in my arms for a moment before I set her back on her feet. When she's standing, I realize she's at least half a foot shorter than me. Now that we're no longer locked together by our lips, I can get a better look at her.

Blond curls. Small nose. Her full, pink lips are swollen from our kiss. Short. Curvy like a mountain road. Her dress barely contains her breasts and strong thighs reveal themselves below the short hem.

My hands rest against her round ass. I spread my fingers to cup more of the soft flesh as I think about lifting the hem to skim the skin where ass becomes leg. I don't know if the area has a name, but it's always been one of my favorite spots on a woman's body. The border between decent and forbidden.

She pushes me away and lurches in the direction of the front door. I see her wobble on her heels as she tries to cut through the rowdy throng. She's either repulsed by me or going to be sick. Neither bodes well for getting her into my bed tonight.

Doing the gentlemanly thing, I shove my way in front of her and take her hand to navigate our escape. We lose contact as people surge in the opposite direction.

"Fuck this," I mumble mostly to myself. This is like trying to drag a sled through sloppy afternoon slush. I grab blondie around the waist and hoist her over my shoulder. "Come on, Tiny Dancer, let's get out of here."

She giggles. I think she asks if I called her Tony, but the noise and her head near my ass make it impossible to hear her clearly.

Chad salutes me as we exit. "Going full caveman tonight, Hayes?"

"He's rescuing me from the zombie hordes," a voice says behind me.

"What the lady said." I turn so he can see her face.

"Carry on. Don't forget protection!" He steps aside to let us out.

I flip Chad the finger over my shoulder.

Outside, I slide blondie to the ground, making sure she's steady before releasing her. "Better?

She sways for a second as she shakes her head no, then nods.

"Are you going to be sick?" I take a step away.

"Probably not. At least not right now. I don't think." She brushes a strand of hair off the flushed skin of her forehead.

I take a step away just in case. "You put on a big show back there. Are you a professional?"

Her eyes widen. "Like a pole professional? Did you just call me a stripper?"

Fuck. "No, not if you think it's a bad thing."

Embarrassment makes my neck itch and I can feel my skin

heat. "You've got moves. I meant it to be flattering. Take it as a compliment. You were the best dancer on the bar tonight. And hella brave, too, with the crowd dive. You're either crazy or trusting to expect someone to catch you."

I stop talking and she keeps staring at me with a funny frown on her face. "I'm sorry for inferring you're a stripper. No harm, no foul?"

She blinks back at me a few times but doesn't answer. I realize she's staring at my mouth. Maybe she's thinking about kissing me again. I'm up for anything involving her mouth.

"I'm Jesse, by the way." I stick out my hand in greeting like we're about to conduct a job interview.

Nothing. If we were in a cartoon, she might be hallucinating me as a steak right now from the hungry look in her eyes.

"Hey, you okay?" I wave my other hand in front of her face. "Hello?"

Her eyes finally meet mine. "Sorry. I was thinking about cake and Canadians."

I chuckle at the non-sequitur. "Makes sense why I lost you for a while."

She grips my T-shirt and sighs happily. "I'm a little tipsy. Sorry."

"For the petting or drinking too much?"

"I'm so sorry, sorry. Sorry." She emphasizes each apology with a pat to my pecs. Blush colors her face when she realizes what she's doing. As she steps away, she says "Sorry," one more time.

If this were a drinking game and I had to take a shot every time she says the word, we'd both be drunk. As it is, I've had only two beers and I'm feeling more sober by the minute.

"Hey," I still her hands, "I didn't say I didn't like it."

Her eyes flash up to mine before she stares at my chest. "It's really nice."

She shivers. In only her party dress, no coat to be seen, she has to be freezing. "Where's your coat? Please tell me you aren't running around in winter without a coat."

"I need to go find my friend." She's still speaking to my chest.

"Dark hair? Tall?" I hold my hand to my chin. "About this tall."

She mimics the height with her own hand. "The spawn of a supermodel and a giraffe?"

"Yeah, I remember her. She was yelling at you as I carried you through the crowd."

"I hope it was about my virtue."

A laugh rolls through my chest. "Not exactly. More like not to bring you back until morning and you have condoms in your purse."

She presses her forehead against my chest. "I need new friends."

"Sounds to me like you have the best kind of friends. The kind who have your back but don't judge you."

"Pushy pusher people." She lifts her head and a small crease forms between her eyes as she stares at my mouth.

Feeling self-conscious, I rub my lips together. She must take this as an invitation for round two because she arches up as tall as she can get and kisses me again.

No, I'm not complaining as she presses her soft curves against me. Her feet tangle with mine and she stumbles. I hold her hips to steady her. Taking my touch as encouragement, she shifts closer and rubs herself against me. It's completely hot, but I attempt to shift away, fully aware we're standing outside a bar with an audience.

Her laughter breaks our kiss. I brush my lips against her cheek and whisper in her ear, "What's so funny?"

"It's too ridiculous." She grips my glutes like a pair of grapefruits she's testing for ripeness. "You'll think I'm a pervert."

Too late. "You're grabbing my ass and you already petted my pecs. I think your pervert status is established. We're making out and you don't even know my name."

"You don't know mine either." Her posture straightens and she sounds defensive.

"I tried to introduce myself and you stared at me like you were starving and I was a cheeseburger."

"Mmm, cheeseburger." She licks her lips and I feel my dick get hard.

"Are you picturing me as food?"

"No, that would be weird." She extends her hand. "I'm Mara."

"Jesse." I wait for the Springfield joke. "Don't say it."

Her forehead wrinkles and she whispers, "I can't say your name. Out loud?"

She's ridiculously cute.

"I said my name out loud when I told you."

"I'm confused. Are you a villain like He Who Shall Not Be Named?"

Instead of continuing to spin in her circular conversation, I tuck her under my arm and hug her. She fits perfectly against my body despite the height difference.

"If you're feeling better, we can go back inside. Or . . ." I let the suggestion go unspoken.

"No."

"Okay. We'll go find your friend. I don't want to leave you out here on your own."

"Afraid the big, bad wolf will come attack me?"

"I'm more worried for the wolf." I don't think she's as bombed as I first thought, but she's definitely at the point of lowered inhibitions if our kissing is anything to go by. I like her and if she's not leaving with her friends, I want her to leave with me.

"Let's go someplace else." She surprises me with her suggestion. "How about your house?"

"My place?" I lift an eyebrow in question and press my lips together. "It's down valley. Too far for just a drink."

"Okay." She agrees as if I suggested it.

I give up fighting my smile. "What exactly are you agreeing to?"

"Whatever. However these things go, I'm up for it. How does this normally work?" She looks eager. The confidence from earlier has faded, but she's keeping up the façade.

"Huh?"

"You pick up a woman and . . . What happens next?"

"Are we speaking hypothetically? Or are you asking for a timeline?" Her questions sound innocent, but her delivery is more straightforward than most women I've met, making for an intriguing combination.

"First, you're the one who jumped into my arms and started kissing me. Second, why do you think I do this on a regular basis?" I ask.

She snorts loudly at the last part.

"You don't even know me." I want to tell her she has me confused for my brothers. I'm the quiet one. The responsible one.

Her apology is mumbled.

"What?" I cup my hand around my ear.

"I made assumptions based on the kissing and your hands on my ass."

"Most of that was you. I followed your lead." I hold up my hands. "I'm an innocent bystander who found himself in the wrong place."

She studies me while chewing on her bottom lip.

She's adorable. "Or a lucky guy in the right place at the right time."

Her confidence must return by the spark in her eyes and

the sassy smile on her face.

"Or that."

I grin down at her.

She continues talking, "We could go back to our condo. It's not far. You could carry me piggyback and probably won't even get winded."

"Someone should make sure you get home safely."

She switches the conversation to dancing. I don't dance. Not since an unfortunate junior high dance where my enthusiasm resulted in ripping my pants.

Ignoring her pleas, I change the subject. "Looks like someone got her second wind."

"One hundred percent. I have amazing rebound skills." She wiggles her eyebrows to let me know she's not only referring to drinking. She's as subtle as a billboard.

And yet I find her charming. I need to know more about her before continuing down the slippery slope into bed. I ignore the sexual overtone of her rebound comment and ask something more personal.

"Is that what this is all about? Some guy back home break your heart?"

Her nose wrinkles and she shakes her head. "So last year's news."

"You're single?" I need her to confirm it. I usually practice don't ask, don't tell with the ski bunnies, but she's different. I don't want to be a side piece, even if it's only for one night.

"Single as the Beyoncé song." She wiggles her fingers at me. "Nobody's put a ring on it. Let's have some fun."

I open my mouth to ask what she means and she kisses me again. Her enthusiasm is contagious and I'm curious to see where the night takes us.

Grinning down at her, I tap her nose with my index finger. "Come on, let's get out of here."

Her eyes widen and she freezes. "Hold that thought!"

When she runs back inside the bar, I'm left standing alone outside, semi-hard and completely confused.

Normally, I take the lead with women. I make the first move and I'm the one who does the seducing. Mara hasn't given me the chance.

No woman has ever had me so worked up with only a kiss. Ever. Lust buzzes through my blood, which is quickly settling in my dick. Beyond the base physical reaction, she makes me laugh and I'm sure I have a stupid grin on my face. It's been months since I've felt like doing either. For the first time in a long time, I want to get to know someone. She's sparked a passion inside of me I thought had disappeared. The chemistry we share with our clothes on promises mind-blowing sex.

THIRTEEN

MARA

JESSE KISSED ME.

Even though it's late in Boston, I call my friend Sofie on the drive home from Aspen.

Jesse kissed me again.

Sofie picks up right before I'm about to give up. "Let me guess, you didn't get laid."

"Why would you assume such a thing?"

Jesse kissed me.

She yawns. "Because you're calling me. What time is it?"

"Late. I went to the movies."

And the hot guy from two years ago kissed me out of nowhere in the middle of a restaurant. He might have a famous girlfriend, but he still kissed me.

"Dinner and a movie sounds like a lovely, respectable, and boring first date."

"I went to the movies with another guy."

Who kissed me in front of the awful date.

"You double-dipped? Who is this pretending to be Mara?"

"I'm not going to look that up on Urban Dictionary to confirm, but I'm confident I can say no."

The kiss tonight was just as amazing as I remember from two years ago. Maybe better because this time I was fully sober. He kissed me.

"Do you like the movie man?"

I fan myself. She can't see me. "Um . . ."

I haven't told her about Jesse because I don't know what to say.

"Do you at least like him more than the excuse to get crepes? I'm guessing yes, since you went to the movies with him after dinner."

I give her the recap of the date disaster, but leave out the kiss. I'm not sure why. I feel protective of the moment, like a tiny speckled egg in a nest.

"Life is too short for bad dates, Mara."

"I think this was the universe reminding me. No more."

"Tell me about the second act. I notice you didn't answer me when I asked if you like him."

"I can't decide. He's hot and cold with me."

Jesse's dimpled smile and gorgeous eyes are warm. The kiss was insane, but then he sat next to me in a movie without touching me again. Honestly, even being close to him and not touching, was hot. Nothing cold about the man.

Then we parted ways after with nothing more than a wave and a reminder about his offer of ski lessons. Not hot. Plus, the Willow Cross canoodling. I want to ask, but haven't. Mostly because I'm a wimp. Same reason I haven't told him we've met before.

"Better than tepid." Sofie yawns through the words.

I'm lost in thoughts about the kiss and how he stared at me during the movie. He's the king of mixed signals.

"Mara? Are you still there?"

"I went out with Jesse." I exhale the relief of sharing the truth with someone.

"Ah, movie guy has a name."

"Yes, it's Jesse."

"I caught that part."

"No. He's Jesse." I wait for the two-year-old lost shoe to drop on her head.

She yawns. "Nice name. If you go out, you'll be his girl. Are you prepared for the Springfield jokes?"

I growl with exasperation. "He's Jesse from the note. Two years ago? My one-night stand disaster?"

This is the first time I've said the words out loud to anyone since running into him and making the connection.

"Hold the phone." She laughs. "I guess I already am. You randomly ran into him again at dinner?"

"Not exactly."

"You've been holding out on me."

"It's only been a couple of weeks since I saw him."

"What?" her voice shrieks through the car's speakers. "Tell me everything. What did he say when he saw you again?"

I explain the entire rescue on the mountain and the helmet gift. I still don't mention the kiss. "He has no idea who I am. Or remembers we may or may not have had drunken sex."

She hums for a moment, then pauses. "You need to refresh his memory."

The kiss should've done that.

Stupid fairy tale magic.

"How? Dive on him from a bar top? Invite him to my bedroom, then pass out?"

"Those are options, but why don't you do the whole 'you look familiar' act and see what he says?"

"We've hung out multiple times. Isn't it too late?" Yes, I'm qualifying the grocery store spying and parking lot loitering as hanging out together. We spent time talking and laughing. It's one of my better dates as of late. Much better than sitting across from Landon.

"Figure it out. If he's hot and single, you should take advantage of life presenting you with a second chance."

Sofie's deep when she's half asleep. "Get this sorted out before my visit. I want him to bring along cute friends for me."

"I'll see what I can do."

We sign off as I make the turn down the lane to the ranch.

The almost full moon shines bright in a cloudless sky. The snow glitters in the semi-darkness and there's enough light to cast shadows.

I inhale the crisp, tart night and exhale a puff of warm air.

For a night that started out terribly, it ended pretty well.

Sitting next to Jesse for hours in the dark might be the best kind of torture I can imagine.

You can do better.

His words echo in my head. He never did give me a straight answer about what he meant.

Better than Landon? Well, that's obvious.

Better than being alone?

Better than him?

I'm still mulling it over as I let out Tapper for his pre-bed ritual. He hop-walks along the fence of the goat pen, casting a shadow against the snow. Not one to dawdle when it's freezing, he beats me back to the door. Inside, Fred and George are each asleep on one of the pillows on my bed. Tapper hops up and takes his place on the blanket at the foot of the bed. They all look cozy enough I hate to move them, but I'm the adult in this family. I'm the only one with opposable thumbs. Sometimes I need to remind myself who's in charge.

You can do better.

Jesse's right. I can do better.

I didn't move here to be boring and waste time with people I don't like.

I can do better.

I press my fingers against my lips, still feeling the lingering press of his mouth.

Much better.

I'm wearing a sombrero and my head is being shaken by a well-endowed woman in a lovely, multi-color dress.

No, I'm not on vacation in Mexico.

It's Taco Tuesday night at the Cantina in Snowmass.

Apparently, taco night involves tequila shooters, which require another person to violently shake my head after each shot.

I've entered the girl bonding phase of being new to town.

When Mae texted and invited me to their weekly tradition, I happily said yes, and here we are. Dinner's over and the energy shifts to a party atmosphere. The bartender cranks up the music and a few people dance near the bar.

Sage and her best friend Zoe join us. Where Sage is pale and bohemian with lavender tips in her hair, Zoe is the dark to her light. More curvy like me, Zoe has long dark hair and dark eyes.

Most of our conversation tonight has centered around Zoe and her boyfriend, Neil. He's starting to talk about moving home to Chicago and she wants to stay. Zoe works as a massage therapist. Sage teaches barre classes and works at Cheeks, a lingerie shop. She says she does it for the discount, but I know from the ranch she's loaded. Mae grew up here and is back for the season to snowboard, waiting tables at La Belle Femme at night.

Everyone has a current gig to make life here possible. The girls sympathize and bemoan the reality of trying to make a life in a resort town. Long-term relationships are tough here. Mae and I are solidly single. Sage has been with Lee for almost a year, so they're still in the honeymoon phase.

"Have you seen Lee?" Mae asks me. Tonight her hair is in two braids wrapped around her head. She looks like the kind of woman who can master everything she finds on Pinterest on her first attempt. Her sweater might be handmade. By her.

"We've only met once," I say.

"He's dreamy." Zoe sighs, and we all nod.

"Much better without his man bun." Sage gets a dreamy, unfocused look to her eyes. "Which is worse for me. Women throw themselves at him right in front of me."

"Hot guys around here all have the same problem," Zoe says. "Women come into town, looking for a one-night stand to check off a box on their fantasy list."

I almost raise my hand and plead guilty. "What about Jesse? Ski patrol?"

Yes, I'm asking if he's a manwhore.

"Hayes? Nah. Maybe a few years ago, but now he keeps to himself, his dog, and old friends." Mae stares at me like she knows exactly why I'm asking the question.

He called Willow an old friend. Is this code for something more?

"More shots," Sage shouts. "Enough talk of men. This is girls' night."

I wave off the lovely waitress with her bottles. "I'm good."

"Do you know why Taco Tuesdays are girls only nights?" Sage yells over the music.

My brain still sloshes around in my head after the shot. "No, why?"

"Because of the pink taco." She solemnly nods as if she's sharing Illuminati level secrets with me. "Think. About. It."

I do. I try, but have you ever had a shooter and then tried to think? The two are mutually exclusive. You'd have better luck pushing magnets together with the same poles facing each other.

Mae puts me out of my misery. "Taco is a euphemism for vagina."

I snort. Okay, this definitely puts a different spin on the C

U Next Tuesday saying.

Whoa, maybe there *is* a shadow society and it's run by women.

I'm still giggling when Zoe declares the evening moon to be full.

"You know what this means, ladies." She stares at each of us in turn, finally locking eyes with me last.

I have no idea. Do we strip off our clothes and howl at the moon?

"Hot tub hijinks!" the rest of the women cheer in unison.

"What?" My voice comes out in a screech.

"Come on, say you'll join us." Sage's genuine happiness shines through her smile. "It's completely silly, but we always have a fun time. Please come."

"Okay," I agree, because she's nice and I'm trying to keep my promise to myself.

FOURTEEN

MARA

"ARE YOU SURE we're not going to get arrested?" I whisper while Mae climbs the fence surrounding the hotel pool and hot tub. "Can't we pretend we're guests and lost our key?"

"Amateur move. They'll never give out a replacement key if we don't show ID matching the reservation." She hops down on the far side, silent and stealthy like a ninja-cat woman.

A quick turn of the lock and the remaining three of us stumble through the opening, shushing each other's giggles with louder voices than the laughter. The only illumination of the area comes from the small landscape lights along the perimeter. Neither the pool nor the hot tub are lit up. Better for trespassers like us.

Mae helps Sage pull the insulation cover from the hot tub. "Come on, we can change and grab towels in the pool house."

Steam rises from the large circle of water like a witch's cauldron.

Or a soup pot.

I shudder and tell myself a five-star hotel must run daily chemical checks.

Of course they must.

Daily.

This isn't a no-tell motel outside the Vegas strip.

Losing my bravado, I hesitate while the other women weave their way around the pool to change.

"What are we changing into? I didn't wear a suit under my dress." I eye Mae. "Was I supposed to?"

"No, the whole point is to skinny dip. Or go the two percent route."

She's lost me entirely.

"Like the milk?"

"The good stuff's not completely out, but neither are you fully clothed?" She gives me a hint, which goes over my head.

I stare at her blankly.

With a sigh, she spells it out for me. "You can wear your underwear."

Sage pipes up, "Don't you dare wear good lingerie in chlorine! It'll be ruined forever."

I love that she thinks I have good lingerie. "I live in scrubs and clogs, do you really think I'm wearing fancy French lace underneath it all?"

"You should be." She opens the door to the little building housing the changing rooms. "Come see me at Cheeks and I'll get you set up. Do you have a boyfriend? He'll love it, too . . . but you should get it for yourself."

I shake my head, but as I think of Jesse, I smile.

"Ah, there's someone you like? Then you definitely want to come see me. Think of it as confidence booster." She gives my hand a squeeze. "And you have to tell me who it is. Local? Someone I know?"

I run my finger across my lips, thinking of Jesse's kiss. "Maybe."

"Come by the shop and we'll chat," she whispers as we walk through the doorway.

Inside, we grab towels from the stack by the door and pick out a spot near the cubbies to strip. I keep my eyes on the wall while I debate going full frontal like Michael Fassbender or wimping out with only some side action in the shadows like Ben Affleck.

Sage's French lingerie comment provides my answer. I remove my bra and leave my panties in place. The bra cost a lot more than the multi-pack cotton underwear.

Logical, practical, and economical.

Breaking and entering is enough spontaneity for one night. Or year.

Hell, it's one of the craziest things I've done in my twenties besides move to the mountains.

Towels tucked around us, we scamper over to the hot tub, avoiding the areas of snow and shiny patches of ice.

The hot tub bubbles away, white froth churning on the surface. I stick a toe into the water and the heat is almost painful in contrast to the cold night air.

"Trust me, you'll be swimming in the pool later to cool off." Zoe gives me an encouraging smile as she sits on the edge.

I join her, swinging my legs in the hot water while I build up the courage to lose my towel.

The sound of male voices on the other side of the metal fence sends me into a panic. I toss my towel and sink into the water up to my chin. Although I'm five seconds from submerging myself and seeing how long I can hold my breath, I have to admit, the water does feel amazing.

I look around and see three similar faces full of surprise. We're like a pack of otters or seals with only our heads visible above the surface. Wide, wild eyes meet mine from multiple directions.

We may be hidden by the edge of the hot tub, but four white towels lay on the decking like a sudden rapture has taken place poolside.

Luckily the voices fade away. False alarm.

Mae's the first to sit up again. "Phew. I would've been bummed to get busted so early."

I laugh. "You sound like getting caught is a certainty."

She and Zoe nod. "We almost always do."

"You've been arrested for public indecency multiple times?" I realize my voice must carry over the water because I hear a faint edge of panic echo back to me. Above the water, this is a G-rated group. We all could be sporting bandeau bikini tops.

"Who said anything about getting arrested?" Sage confidently rests her arms along the edge of the hot tub, exposing the top of her breasts.

"But Mae said you get caught." I make sure my own boobs remain submerged.

"Oh, sure. We're sent home with a warning not to do it again by whichever poor sap is on night duty at the hotels."

"Or club," Zoe adds. "However, they're a little more touchy about non-members usurping member privileges."

"Sometimes we know the person who is tasked with kicking us out. Can be a little awkward, because of the whole nudity thing, but usually we end up laughing about it over drinks at some point."

"I'm surrounded by outlaws and miscreants," I mumble. I have no one to blame but myself. I'm the responsible one. I've never crashed a car or shoplifted. I didn't drink at high school parties or steal money out of my mother's purse. Never broke curfew. Hell, I don't think I was ever grounded at all.

Now I'm running around with exhibitionists flaunting rules and snubbing my nose at the law.

Obviously, the high altitude and lack of oxygen affect my ability to make good choices.

Feeling a little overheated, or maybe I'm having a hot flash,

I decide I need to cool off in the pool. I hold my arm over my chest bashfully as I step out of the hot water into the cool air. The shock of the contrast is refreshing.

I get a few whistles and soft whoops of encouragement from my new friends as I tiptoe across the freezing concrete to the pool. Emboldened, I shake my butt before executing a perfect shallow dive.

I swim the length underwater, enjoying the silence and the feel of my muscles stretching with each stroke. The cool water feels amazing after the heat of the hot tub. At the far end, my head breaks the surface and I gulp air to fill my burning lungs.

With one hand I clutch the edge of the pool, and with the other I swipe water from my eyes. As I face the hot tub blinking away the sting of chlorine, my smile falters when I realize we're no longer alone.

Two men stand between me and my friends.

One of them is Lee.

Okay, that's mortifying.

But not as mortifying as seeing a familiar face on the second guy.

FIFTEEN

JESSE

LEE CONVINCES ME to sneak up on the girls at the hotel pool. There's a full moon tonight and he knows they're up to something when Sage doesn't return his texts. He convinces me to drive him to Snowmass and up to the village.

"Why do you think they're skinny dipping? Isn't it Taco Tuesday?"

He points up at the bright night sky. "Because one of Sage's New Year's resolutions last month involved howling at the moon more often."

"Why does she need to be naked in a hotel hot tub to howl at the moon?" I tilt my head back and let loose a long, low growl before lifting it into a woeful cry.

I half expect a real wolf to reply.

"Keep it down, Hayes. You'll ruin the element of surprise." He pulls me down the path between the hotel and the mountain.

"I admit I feel a little uncomfortable showing up to spy on your naked girlfriend." I stuff my hands in my jacket pockets because I suddenly feel like a third wheel.

"I hadn't really thought about you seeing Sage naked. Don't look at her." Lee says something more and I hear his South

African accent slip through. *"Vokkof."*

He stops short and I bump into him.

"We can turn back. No one will have to know we're here."

He lifts a corner of this mouth in a half smirk. "Or we join them. If everyone is naked, it will be less awkward."

I have no body issues, but his argument wouldn't get us out of jail.

Female voices carry around the corner.

"You still want to do this?" he asks.

"Sure." I nod in agreement, however, I'm not at all sure that's a good idea. "How are we getting in?"

"Sage usually wedges the gate open for a quick escape."

"Usually?" How are there groups of women naked in hot tubs around town on a regular basis and I'm only finding out about it now? I've become too much of a hermit.

We slip into the pool area undetected. I count three heads in the hot tub. None of them are Mara. Maybe she chickened out and went home. My disappointment surprises me.

I spin toward the gasp behind me.

Mara's face ducks down below the edge of the pool.

I stand my ground. I'm between her and the hot tub where the towels are piled next to a huge sombrero. She'll have to surface eventually for air.

Her lung capacity impresses me.

I clap when she pops her head out of the water again. "Twenty-two seconds. I was worried you planned to avoid me all night."

"I'm naked," she whispers.

"Are you?" I tease and lean forward from where my feet are planted. "I can't tell."

Sadly, it's the truth. The pool is dark and the low lights from the surrounding hotel building don't provide enough detail to see anything below the water's surface.

"What are you doing here?" Her teeth chatter from the cold air.

"Lee wanted to come find Sage." I thumb over my shoulder. "You sound cold, you should get out of the pool."

She shakes her head and dips lower into the water.

"It's not a ploy to see you naked. I can hear your teeth chattering from here."

In the low light, I barely see eyebrows rise in doubt.

"I'll close my eyes." I will try not to peek.

"Hand me the sombrero." She adds, "Please."

As I walk over to retrieve the hat, I try to figure out why she wants it. I hold the enormous straw hat in front of me.

"Okay, this is how this is going to go down. Put the sombrero on the ground, then turn around."

I follow her instructions.

"Are your eyes closed?"

"I'm not looking."

"Close 'em." I want to laugh at how serious she sounds.

"Fine." I cover my face with my hands. "Better?"

"No peeking."

While I've fantasized about her being naked and wet, this isn't exactly how I imagined it. For one thing, I'd be naked, too. And for another, we would be alone. Not in public with a bunch of drunk girls and an oversized rugby player.

That sounds a lot kinkier than my imagination could conjure.

A soft splash and the sound of wet feet on pavement tell me she's out of the pool. I resist turning to face her and it takes all my self-control.

"Brrr, it's freezing!"

"Can I turn around now?"

"I think so."

I open my eyes and twist my head to peer at her over my

shoulder. She's holding the sombrero in front of her, covering all the fun parts.

"Nice outfit."

She does a little curtsey, inadvertently giving me a glimpse of the top of her full breasts as she bends. "Back up. I need to get into the hot tub."

"You're very bossy."

"Hurry. Before I get frostbite."

I hop step over to my friends. She's greeted with soft whoops and applause as she manages to reenter the water without more than a peek of skin and a flash of blue panties.

"Ahh, much better." She sinks up to her chin in the bubbling water.

Lee sits on the cement near Sage, with his naked legs in the water like some sort of Greek god in boxer briefs surrounded by water nymphs. "Are you going to join us?"

On a normal crazy night, full moon or not, I wouldn't hesitate, but at the moment I'm sporting a semi hard-on. If I take off my jeans, the evidence will be more than evident.

"Hand me the sombrero."

"Suddenly shy, Jesse?" Zoe teases as she tosses me the hat.

"Just being polite to the new girl." With a wink at Mara, I remove my boots and socks, then strip off my jeans, making sure to keep covered. "Fuck. It's cold."

I manage to get into the water without flashing anyone or poking anyone's eye out. My moan of contentment echoes Mara's. I sit across from her, pretty sure sitting next to her naked might be the death of me. When I catch her staring at my chest, I smirk. Her cheeks are flushed and I don't think the color is only from the heat of the water.

Besides the fact we're all pretty much naked, the conversation isn't awkward. I can see how Mara fits right in with Sage's friends. Knowing she's making connections means she'll be more likely to stay in the area.

If she stays, maybe we have a chance to be more than a failed one-night stand.

I'm not the same party guy I was when we first met years ago. I'd like the chance to prove it.

"I'm going in the pool, if anyone wants to join me." I hoist myself out of the water by bracing my arms on the side.

"You're not even naked," Mara announces.

I give her a smirk, "Neither are you."

"You peeked!"

I shrug and dive into the pool with a smile on my face. When I surface, I see I'm not alone in the water. Mara clings to the side, her chest pressed against the wall. I swim over to her side.

"Sorry." I bump her shoulder with mine.

"We're even. I watched you jump in the pool."

"Oh you did, did you?" I grin down at her.

"You made a spectacle of yourself. How could I not?"

She pushes wet curls away from her face. A few drops of water slide along her cheekbones before falling away. Her full lips are inches from mine. I rest my head against the edge and continue to stare at her.

I'm still thinking about kissing her when the pool lights flash on and off.

Mara squeaks and goes under water again. For a glorious second, I'm looking down at her boobs underwater.

"Party's over," a male voice announces from next to the pool house.

I squint through the dark at the familiar, short, stocky man. "Brandon?"

"Hayes?" He walks closer to the pool. "What the hell are you doing in the pool?"

Mara's head breaks the surface and she inhales a deep breath.

"Oh, that answers my question." He backs away.

"What?" I stare at him, then at Mara. I chuckle. "Not what it looks like. We're swimming."

"Naked in the middle of the night at a hotel where you're not a guest. When are you going to grow up? You're just like Cody."

"Low blow, man." Glowering at him, I lift myself out of the pool. "We weren't having sex in the pool, but you're right, we are trespassing."

"Jesse Hayes got rejected? Lost your touch?" Brandon's smugness oozes out of him. He thinks he's won some contest between us, but he's been the only one competing.

"Come on, Brandon. No harm, no foul." Lee's voice carries over to where we stand. "No reason to bring up the past. We'll gather our stuff and go."

I haven't thrown a punch since Cody was around to instigate fights. Brandon's treading on a thin layer of ice over my self-control.

He stands with his arms crossed. "I'm not going to apologize."

"Fine, but you could be a decent guy and turn your back to let the women get out of the water without getting a free peep show."

You little pervert, I add in my head.

"It's too cold to stand around out here policing you. I'll give you five minutes to leave before I call security."

"I thought you were security," I ask.

"I'm working the overnight shift and saw people on the cameras." He points to the corner of the changing room.

A disgusted snort escapes me. "You are a little perv."

"You want privacy, don't get naked in public."

Sound advice.

"You know sneaking into hot tubs is a tradition around here. Just because you're never invited doesn't mean you get to spy to get material for your spank bank." Sage stands next to me with a towel wrapped around her middle.

Normally, she's all about yoga and Zen, but I never underestimate her.

Lee joins us on her other side. He hands me a towel and I drape it over my shoulders. The three of us create a wall to give the other three some privacy.

"I have no beef with you. As long as you leave, no harm, no foul." He repeats Lee's words back to me in a mocking tone. He gives us a small salute off his forehead. "Have a good evening."

"He's always been a little prick," I grumble as I glare at his retreating back.

"And he loves getting under your skin." Lee slaps me on the back. "Don't let him get to you. He's not worth the energy."

Lee's right. Brandon is a little twerp wannabe. He used to hang around the fringes of Cody's circle growing up. I've always disliked him and never more than tonight for bringing up my brother as a way to insult me while acting like a little cockblocker.

With the girls in the changing room, I walk over to my jeans and then peel off my wet boxers. I slip into my cold jeans and tug on my shirt, grumbling the entire time. Sage can take Lee home. I've had enough fun for the night.

"I'll catch you later," I tell him. "Tell everyone I said bye."

"Hey, we can go for a beer. Don't let Brandon ruin your mood." Lee hands me my jacket.

"Nah, I'm done. Getting too old for this shit."

I'm gone before I can say good-bye to Mara.

SIXTEEN

JESSE

AFTER LAST TUESDAY, I'm not sure if Mara will still show for our ski lesson. Sunday morning promises a gorgeous robin's egg day. Crystalline clear skies, warm sun, and not a lot of wind blowing snow off the peak. Perfect ski conditions.

I think about swinging by the ranch to pick her up, but convince myself to stick to our original plan. So here I am, pacing around the parking lot at the gondola. The lifts don't open for another half hour.

I spot Mara's red helmet weaving through the cars in the lot. She holds two stacked paper cups in one of her gloved hands and balances her skis on her shoulder with the other.

When she sees me, she grins.

"I brought coffee. Figured we can drink it on the gondola." She nods at the top cup. "I have sugar in my pocket if you need it."

"I knew there was a reason we're friends." With a grin, I take the coffee and sip it. "Perfect."

"Are we?" She brings her coffee up to her mouth but doesn't drink it.

"I've seen your boobs. I think we're more than acquaintances."

I nudge her shoulder, hoping she takes the bait.

"Almost a half-dozen people in the greater Roaring Fork valley can say the same thing after Tequila Tuesday. Since when are boobs a qualification of friendship?"

"Who said I wanted to be friends with you?" We set our skis in the rack on the outside of the gondola and step inside.

"You did. Five seconds ago." She sits down and I join her on the same bench.

"I said it made us more than acquaintances."

"Listen, just because you've seen my boobs more than once, doesn't give you special privileges."

"What do you mean more than once? Okay, yes, I looked more than one time, but other than your ill-fated foray into a life of crime the other night, when?"

Her faces scrunches up. "Are you kidding me?"

I shake my head. "I'd remember. Trust me."

"Apparently not."

Now it's my turn for confusion. I feel my brows draw together into a painful V between my eyes. "No, I'd definitely remember. First, because they're beautiful, and second, because they're yours. Pretty sure I could pick them out of a line-up. Or if you sent me a boob pic, I'd know they're yours."

"Despite what men want to think, boob pics aren't a thing most women do. We just don't. Second, you have and you did."

"Refresh my memory." She ignores my eager expression.

"I'm not flashing you in the middle of the gondola."

"We're the only ones in here." I give her puppy eyes. "Come on, I'm not really asking you to show me your boobs right now. That's not what I meant. I have an excellent recall."

"Do you?" She looks doubtful.

I nod. "An almost photographic memory."

Now I'm openly baiting her. After kissing her at La Belle Femme, if she did, wouldn't she say something? Either she doesn't remember or won't admit she kissed me without knowing my name two years ago and I'm tired of pretending it never happened.

We only have a few minutes until we reach Elk Camp. I sip my coffee, letting her stew for a minute. She could melt steel with her stare, but I refuse to face her. Instead, I gaze out the windows at the snowy wonderland below us.

With a huff, she drinks her coffee. In fact, she guzzles it like it's a shot. Maybe her cup has booze and mine is only coffee.

"Unbelievable," she mutters and shifts farther away in the seat from me.

"Mara?" I continue looking out the windows. "If you for one more minute believe I don't remember meeting you at the Onion two years ago, you're a fool. Do you want me to describe our first kiss? Because I can. In detail. You were standing above me on a bar, like a siren calling all the men in the place to you in your sparkly dress. One minute you were unattainable, the next you were kissing me. You made me feel like the luckiest guy in the place. Crazy, unexpected, and I wanted you from the second you landed in my arms."

Her coffee cup hovers near her open mouth as I lean close and lower my voice. "I can still taste the sweetness of your mouth and the feel of your curves in my hands."

I'm close enough to hear her gasp.

"For some reason, you're pretending we've never met before. Either I'm forgettable or you're ashamed. I highly doubt the former is true, and if the latter is the issue, life's too short for shame. I don't regret a single thing about that night. Or kissing you in the restaurant."

She meets my eyes for a brief moment and then studies her cup. "What about Willow?"

"What about her?" I'm confused.

She frowns and won't look at me.

I duck into her sight line. "You've lost me."

"Isn't she your girlfriend?"

A low laugh of disbelief gets stuck in my throat. "Wrong Hayes brother. She's a friend."

"I saw you together in Aspen." She confesses to being in the crowd the night of the party. "You looked . . . close on the red carpet. Then the tabloids called you a couple."

"We've never been anything more than friends." I pick up one of her curls and twist it around my finger. "You ran away before I could introduce you."

Her eyes widen. "Why would you do that?"

"I wanted Willow to meet you." I continue playing with her curl, pulling it straight before releasing it.

"I don't understand."

"I've known her most of my life, but she doesn't come home often. She might be a famous actress now, but she'll always be little foul-mouthed Willow, and my brother Cody's high school girlfriend to me. I can admire her beauty, but she's like a kid sister. Never going to cross that line."

When Mara's confused, an adorable crinkle appears between her eyebrows. "Why would you want *me* to meet her? We just met."

"That's not a hundred percent true." I lean closer, feeling her breath against my mouth.

"Which part?" Her voice is barely above a whisper.

"We hadn't just met. You crashed back into my life." I stare at her lips for a beat and then take her gloved hand in mine. "I do have one regret when it comes to the night we met. I regret leaving in the morning without waking you up and getting your number. At the time I thought life was pointless and the only way to live was in the moment. You weren't going to stay and us ever seeing each other again felt like an impossibility."

"You left a note."

"You do remember." I finally meet her eyes again.

Her tongue wets her bottom lip and she nods.

The tension between us grows with every inhale and unsteady exhale. Unable to resist her, I press a soft kiss against the corner of her mouth.

"I've never had a kiss like that." My lips hover with hers.

"Me neither." Her voice is hushed, lost in memory. "I thought I'd imagined it, but then you kissed me again at the restaurant. I've never been kissed the way you kiss me."

It's all the encouragement I need. I close the distance between us and crash my mouth against hers, enveloping her in my arms. She clutches my shoulders with her gloves. Parting her lips, she slips her tongue into my mouth. She tastes of coffee and the same sweetness I remember. My memory might be good, but it doesn't compare to the reality of kissing her again. I nip her plump bottom lip like I've wanted to do since I escorted her off of the mountain.

Lost in her, I barely notice when the gondola slows. The cold air from the open doors announces our arrival.

"Hold the thought." I give her one last peck on the lips before standing and lifting her by the hand. Giving her my coffee, I collect both our skis and poles.

"Can we skip the brush with death and the adrenaline rushes for more kissing?" she asks as she trails behind me.

Chuckling, I hand over her skis. "No."

She puts on her gloves and clasps her poles. "I know of a much better way to get our blood pumping."

Her wiggling eyebrows make me laugh. "You're adorable."

"Trying to be sexy here." She pushes out her full bottom lip.

Seeing her pout as an invitation, I gently bite her lip. "You're both. Sexy and adorable is a perfect combination."

"You won't think so when I'm a sweaty, incoherent mess in the middle of a panic attack." She's serious.

"I've got you." I push one of her curls away from her face. "I'm not going to let anything happen to you."

Her lids flutter closed and she leans her cheek against my hand. "Promise?"

"Promise." I give her a soft kiss, barely brushing my tongue inside of her mouth.

"Get a room," a group of kids no taller than my elbow shout as they shove past us to get to the slopes.

"Little assholes," I whisper against Mara's lips, unwillingly to let punk elementary kids ruin my moment. "Come on. I promise to make it good for you."

She moans against my mouth and then she stills before opening her eyes. "You mean skiing, don't you?"

"Don't sound so disappointed." After giving her one more peck, I push off on my skis. "Trust me."

I take us down a few blue runs, then we take the lift over to High Alpine. My goal is to build up her confidence on a few easy blues in preparation for a more expert run. I know she can handle it.

There's a short wait for the quad up to Big Burn and I use the opportunity to kiss her in line. She's glowing with confidence after today's skiing. I love seeing her smile and the way her eyes almost close when she really grins. I'm falling for her hard and fast, but can't seem to care.

I fight the urge to end our ski date early and take her somewhere more private. For a brief moment, I even consider bringing her to one of the ski patrol shacks or finding a warming hut on the mountain, but neither of those promise privacy.

Instead, I'll settle for sitting next to her and spending time together in the sun.

"What are your feelings about eating at almost twelve thousand feet?" I ask

"Is this a euphemism for sex?" Her dark lashes flutter in

surprise, but her grin is mischievous.

I choke on nothing and cough out a laugh. "No, I'm talking about pizza. I'm starved."

Embarrassment floods her cheeks with color. "Please ignore that comment."

Once we're on the lift, I give her a quick kiss. "You have a dirty mind."

I swear she mumbles, "If you only knew" under her breath, but when I ask her to repeat it, she refuses.

"I can't wait to find out." Slinging my arm behind her shoulders, I pull her closer.

"Do you know the Mushers Kennel?" Mara asks as she steals my crust. She thinks she's being sly, but I've never been a fan. She's doing me a favor.

We're sitting next to each other in the sun on the deck outside. This day is pretty close to perfect. We've spent an hour getting to know each other, sharing details of where we grew up and our families in between eating and quick kisses. I skip over the details about Cody, focusing the conversation on her stories.

"Everyone in town knows about them. They've been around for decades. Why do you ask?"

"Have you ever visited the kennels?" She dips her stolen crust into a little plastic cup of ranch dressing.

After wadding up my napkin, I toss it on my plate. "No, but they're popular with the tourists. People have a romanticized idea based on the Iditarod and Jack London novels they read as a kid."

"We're working with them to make sure the dogs aren't being abused." Her eyes cloud with the sadness.

"Mistreated? How?" I bristle at the idea of animal cruelty

and sit up straight.

"Not enough rest time, inadequate shelters, untreated injuries, and inbreeding are the typical issues." Her voice switches tone to sound more detached and professional.

"Are you going out there on your own?" I know the family who runs the kennel. They're good people, but probably won't welcome a stranger walking around the property. Like ranchers, they're private folks with an independent streak. They don't trust big government and regulations established by people in big cities who've never set foot in Colorado. Mara would stick out.

"I'll go with you. We can drive out there tomorrow."

"Why do you think I need an escort?" She wipes her hands on a napkin.

"Going with a local might get you more information than you showing up there as a stranger. We take our privacy seriously out here. And a lot of us like our guns."

Her eyes widen. "You think I'd get shot?"

"No, but I've know the family for years. I'll make the introductions."

"I wasn't nervous about asking questions until you brought up the guns."

"We'll be fine. They're good people."

Who better be treating their dogs right. Or they'll have more than Mara and Elizabeth to answer to.

She sips her hard cider and leans against the deck railing in the sun. Her golden hair almost glows against the bright blue of the sky.

"Are you staring at me?" she asks with her eyes closed.

"Totally. You're beautiful." I rest my head next to hers.

"I'm glad you remember me." She opens one eye and squints at me.

"I can't believe you thought I didn't."

She leans her head closer to mine. "I have a question."

Our noses brush we're so close together. "Ask me."

"It's embarrassing."

"I'm not easily shocked. Tell me. Maybe I have the answer."

"Have we had sex?" she whispers, her focus on my mouth.

Whatever I thought she would ask me, it wasn't that. Why would she . . .

"You don't know?" I'm stunned. How, what, huh, what? Why would she think we've had sex? The truth drops on me like a boulder. "You don't remember."

"It's kind of a blur," she confesses, shy and clearly embarrassed.

For two years, I've been dreaming of her kiss while she's been thinking we had sex and she can't remember it. I'm going to have to fix this soon.

"We didn't have sex." I kiss her soft lips. "I promise when we do, you'll remember it."

SEVENTEEN

Two Years Ago

MARA

"MARA."

"SHH. YOU'LL wake him."

"Mara."

"Shh. Go away. We're naked."

"Who's naked?"

"Quit yelling. You'll wake him up."

"Mara. You're dreaming. Open your eyes." A delicate, not manly hand jostles my shoulder.

"I'm not and I won't. You're interrupting."

The hand tugs off the duvet.

Screaming, I roll over to cover my lover.

I land on cool sheets and nothing but the mattress. Flipping to my back, I cover my boobs and cross my legs. My hands touch cotton fabric. At least I'm not naked.

Finally opening my eyes, I'm greeted with an empty bed and my best friend, Sofie, laughing her ass off.

"Wow. You must have been having one sexy dream," she barks out between laughs.

I peer over the side of the bed.

"Where'd he go?" The closed en suite door catches my attention.

After scrambling off of the bed, I tiptoe over to the door. I press my ear against the wood to listen for signs of life inside.

"What are you doing?" she half speaks, half laughs.

I wave my arm behind me in the universal gesture of "shut your cakehole so I can snoop."

Nothing. No running water. No mouth-breathing sounds.

With a light tap on the door, I turn the handle while speaking. "Occupato, Mr. Roboto?"

What's wrong with me?

The handle gives easily and I swing open the door to an empty room.

Empty except for my clothes from last night in the shower and a big heart drawn on the mirror with the letters J and M in the middle.

"Is that lipstick?" Sofie, being an Amazon, peers over my head. "It better not be my Nars."

The color does look like Jilted Love.

How appropriate.

I put down the lid and sit on the toilet. My clothes lie in a sad, damp pile. "What happened?"

Sofie frowns at me. "You're asking me? You don't remember?"

I shake my head. "It's all a little blurry. I swear I brought a guy back with me, but apparently not."

"Hold on." She leaves the bathroom. I hear her footsteps disappear down the hall.

I jump up and close the door so I can pee in private. Brushing my teeth would be a good idea, too. I'm not sure why, but my mouth tastes like Fruit Loops, wool, and vodka.

Not a great mix.

I stare at my reflection, expecting to see a hot mess, but am greeted by a clean face. No raccoon eyes. No smeared lipstick. Instead of a sad clown, I look pretty normal.

Huh.

Sometimes I amaze myself.

Splashing water on my face, I try to piece together the wee hours of the night.

Despite being convinced I was naked in bed with a man when I woke up, I'm wearing a tank top and my own underwear.

My cheeks have a little beard burn on them, but there's no other physical sign of a hook up.

I do a mental body check. No weird marks. Or hickeys.

I've never blacked out from drinking.

Or had sex and not been able to remember.

In all honesty, I've never had a one-night stand before.

I hope if last night was my first, I'd remember.

Retracing the evening's events, I start at the Onion.

Dancing on the bar.

Diving into the crowd.

Strong arms catching me.

Kissing the gorgeous tall man attached to those arms.

It was a helluva kiss.

He was my kissing soul mate.

I know I didn't imagine that part.

Then we were outside, mostly talking. Less kissing.

An encore bar.

More dancing.

This time not on a bar.

Close together.

Like having sex standing up with our clothes on.

I remember a tiny, crowded dance floor in a dark club pulsing with bodies and loud music.

More kissing.

Making out against a door.

Inviting him inside for sex.

Because that was my mission.

I glance in the trash for a telltale sign we had the sex.

The basket is empty except for a few balled-up tissues and a kazoo.

I definitely do not remember the kazoo part of the evening.

I leave the bathroom to search the bedroom, then return for toilet paper. If there's a condom lying around, I don't want to touch it.

Sofie finds me on my hands and knees beside the bed. The duvet and pillows sit on the dresser.

"What are you doing?"

"Looking for evidence."

"Of?"

"Sex."

"Do you want a blacklight?"

We meet eyes and both shudder.

"Wouldn't you know?"

"You'd think, but I can't tell."

"You weren't naked, and you were alone when I found you."

"I think he left in the middle of the night."

"Like dine and dash?"

"More like screw and scram."

"Or fuck and flee."

"This isn't making me feel any better."

I collapse on the unmade bed.

"Here, I brought you coconut water and drugs."

"I've told you, just because pot is legal in Colorado doesn't mean I'm going to turn into a stoner."

"It's ibuprofen. But I do have some edibles left we need to eat before we board the plane. Or lose them forever."

I repeat her last sentence in my head. "I did have a guy here last night. I quoted *Top Gun* at him. Then begged him to end my dry spell."

"Sounds romantic."

"The greatest love story ever told." This is the moment I'd like to bury my head under a pillow, or five, but can't because I stripped the bed. Instead, I groan and throw my arm over my face.

"Either I had unprotected and terrible sex with a micro penis. Or I failed at Operation Fun Time Mara."

"I have video from last night saying otherwise. You were most definitely fun time Mara earlier in the evening."

"Maybe I peaked too early. You can lead a thoroughbred to the mare, but you can't force him to do the deed."

"I thought you didn't even like horses." She sounds as confused as I am by the weird turn our conversation has taken.

"I don't." I stare at her blankly.

"Speaking of horses, tell me more about last night." Her eyebrows do a little dance on her forehead as she makes a lame attempt at innuendo.

I hate to squash her hopes and dreams of good dirt with my inability to remember, or more importantly, feel, anything from last night. "Non stallion status."

"Boo. He was all big hands and long limbs. How deceitful."

"Leave it to me to have a one-night stand and not be able to remember the details."

"Are you sure you had sex?" She sits down next to me. "I'm a little worried you can't recall any details."

Dread settles low in my belly. "Do you think I was roofied?"

"You know, I like to see the best in people and walk on the sunny side of life, but you weren't *that* drunk when you left the bar with him."

"I almost hurled on his shoes. I think it's possible I passed out or fell asleep before the good stuff."

Our friend Nina walks into my room holding a piece of

paper. She looks like I feel, all messy eye makeup and silly string in her hair. "Who's Jesse?"

"The micro-penis I tried to have sex with last night?" I can't bother to lift my head.

"Well, he left you a note on the coffee table." She waves the paper around. I pretend to reach for it from the bed.

"What does it say?"

Sofie intervenes and steals it from Nina. "Thanks for a memorable night. I haven't laughed so hard in a long time."

I groan.

Sofie snickers. "Laughter doesn't sound like a hot time."

"Is there more?"

She continues reading, "I hope you're not too hungover this morning. I stayed as long as I could. Sorry about your clothes. J."

Nina lies down next to me. "Doesn't sound like a post-sex note to me."

"What does he mean by your clothes?" Sofie asks

"Everything's in a heap in the shower."

"Are you sure you didn't throw up?" Nina leans away from me like I'm contagious.

I press my fists against my eyes. "I don't think so. There isn't any evidence."

Vague memories of kissing in a fountain flit through my head. Not a fountain. More like a hose, or spray. None of it clicks together into a cohesive timeline.

Sofie pets my hair. "At least you didn't imagine him here. You have proof of life."

"I didn't kidnap him. He came willingly. I think."

Nina scoffs. "The coming is the big mystery, isn't it?"

"We're not going to figure out Mara's mysterious night if she can't give us more details, and her prince charming is MIA." Sofie pats my shoulder.

"Did he steal one of your shoes so he'll be able to find you again?" Nina asks.

"He wasn't a weirdo." I'm mostly confident in the truth of this statement. I think. Maybe.

"The note is a nice touch, but doesn't negate the potential for being a weirdo."

"Nina, your law school is showing. Can we stop arguing the evidence and forget it ever happened?" Shame and embarrassment begin to creep into my head. Tears fill the corner of my eyes and slip into my hair.

"Oh, Mara."

"Can we never speak of this again?" I swipe away the tears. "Let's pretend I had the time of my life and multiple orgasms."

"Maybe he screwed you stupid."

"Nina!" Sofie and I shout at the same time.

"What? I'm trying to be helpful. Maybe the sex was incredibly, off the charts, hot and you lost brain cells because of all of the orgasms."

Biologically, it's not possible, but I like her idea better than a failed one-night stand or unmemorable sexing.

EIGHTEEN

MARA

MY TRUTHS ARE untrue.

"We didn't have sex. I promise when we do, you'll remember it."

I'm not sure if I should be relieved or frustrated, embarrassed or happy we didn't have sex two years ago. I've been walking around thinking life is one way with certain truths and facts, but it's all been a lie.

I'm relieved sex with Jesse didn't suck. I'm frustrated I can't remember the rest of the night.

I'm embarrassed I had to ask him.

Then he goes and says when we have sex. Not if. When.

I gulp the rest of my hard cider.

How soon is when? Now?

I seriously consider dragging him into the bathroom right over there. Hell, we can find a private spot behind a tree. Although these ski clothes might make it impossible to get busy. Plus, snow is cold.

While he kisses me, I have a whole conversation in my head about where on this mountain we can have sex.

I squeeze my legs together to keep myself from moaning. The pressure relieves the urge to mount him.

Public mounting is probably frowned upon in Aspen. At least before noon and if neither the mounter or the mountie is famous. Or loosely related to someone famous. Or a Kardashian. Or any number of hotel heiresses.

I don't think Jesse falls into this category, but Aspen is a ski town, so his brother's fame might count.

What am I thinking? I'm rationalizing attacking him in the middle of the day. In front of families with children. In front of strangers. Everything about the idea is wrong, but I'm still not entirely convinced it's a bad one. I imagine things get pretty wild during après ski around here. It's three o'clock somewhere.

Before I do something that might get us arrested, or him fired, I break away from his kiss.

I straighten my spine and pretend we weren't making out two seconds ago.

Inhaling slowly, I calm my racing heart.

"Don't you ever get tired of skiing?" I dip my stolen pizza crust into my ranch dressing like we've just been sitting here chatting, not letting our lust run wild.

His silence brings my eyes up to meet his warm, golden brown eyes. Honestly, he looks a little flushed and his lips are a deeper rose against the copper-flecked dark scruff.

"Do you get tired of breathing? Or waking up every morning alive?" He sits up and drinks the rest of his beer. At this altitude, the sun is strong enough, he's peeled off his jacket and pushed up the sleeves of his T-shirt.

I laugh before realizing he's serious.

"Please don't say breathing is overrated." He licks a little drop of ranch dressing off of the side of my thumb. No, he sucks the skin into his mouth and his tongue darts out to finish the job.

I replay the action in my head a few times.

Yep, totally dirty.

Maybe my food is drugged. Or the ginger snap I ate earlier was no ordinary cookie. Okay, it wasn't, but I needed something to help calm my anxiety over skiing again. There's a shop in Aspen with yummy edibles, aka an anxious girl's best friends.

"Are you okay?" His voice breaks through the crazy thoughts running unfettered in my head. "You're flushed and have a wild look in your eyes."

I finish off my glass of ice water in a few large gulps. "Fine. Why?"

With the corner of my napkin, I dab my chin. "Do I have something on my face?"

He gestures to the corner of his own mouth. "Something right there."

I swipe the napkin over the spot on my lips, but it comes away clean. Repeating the motion, I stare at him. "Did I get it?"

He leans closer, close enough I can see flecks of amber in the warm caramel of his eyes. "My bad. I think it was drool."

Did he seriously just play me?

"What would I be drooling over?"

"Me." There's not a second of hesitation in his voice. "Of course."

"Wow. Arrogant much?"

"Stating the facts." His normally sweet smile has a gloating edge to it. He's showing too many teeth.

"Which are what?" I narrow my eyes at him.

"You think I'm hot." Hell yes, I'm not blind.

"Don't get too full of yourself. I was drinking water. I can see how the two could be easily confused."

"Right." The dimple of suppressed amusement makes its appearance.

"Is your ego so delicate you need me to be your personal fluffer?" I pretend to fluff a pillow.

His eyes widen. "You need to stop."

"Why?"

"It's obscene." He tries to grab my hands.

I repeat the gesture with both hands. "How?"

"Not whatever you're doing with your hands. The word fluffer. It's a dirty job." He presses his lips together.

"Like the show where the guy goes and does disgusting things people do for work?"

"No, like in porn." He's trying not to laugh and about a second from failing.

My hands still mid-air. Now it looks like I'm groping imaginary boobs. I drop them into my lap and sit on them to avoid any further levels of mortification.

"This is going well." Embarrassment rises from my chest up my neck to my cheeks.

Jesse apparently thinks so because he's full-out laughing now. The man tosses his head back and lets laughter roar out of him.

At my expense.

"Can you keep it down a little? I'm trying to die a quiet, respectable death here and now people are staring." I poke him in the side.

He takes a moment or two to regain control of his laughter. Each time I think he's done, another chuckle bursts out of him like a bubble rising to the surface of a champagne flute.

His shoulders tremble with amusement as he tries to look me in the eye. I swear his face deepens with color as he attempts to hold in the laughter.

"Go on, then. Don't burst something trying to contain it. Let it out before you hurt yourself." I give up the last shred of my dignity.

When he kisses me, his shoulders still shake from aftershocks, but I don't mind because his tongue is in my mouth doing magical things.

NINETEEN

MARA

IF SLOTH IS my vice, patience is most definitely not my virtue.

We kissed and canoodled all over the mountain on Sunday. It was heavenly torture.

He walked me to my car and kissed me stupid in the parking lot. Yes, I was still wearing my helmet.

Then he left me high and dry again with a promise he'd make it worth the wait. The way he lowered his voice and whispered the words against my ear like he was telling me a secret made me want to risk arrest and jump him in public. Again.

I'm about to explode from sexual frustration.

I'm not a people doctor, but I am a medical professional, so I can say with some authority dying from horniness might be possible.

Now we're trapped together in his Land Cruiser on a visit to the Mushers Kennel.

Jesse's talk about guns and anti-city people sentiments has me nervous as we drive down a private, unpaved road marked with No Trespassing, Private Property, and No Hunting signs along the open wood fencing. Keep out. Got it.

We pass a pen with small kennels and about two dozen

barking dogs. They're creating a ruckus but their body language is excited, not fearful. From the window, I see loose tails and ears up, no raised hackles. I'll take it as a good sign.

Elizabeth called and set up the meeting, so we're not arriving unexpected. Part of me wanted the element of surprise so they couldn't hide any evidence of wrongdoing. However, when Jesse brought up his concerns, I'm grateful we have an appointment.

The barking and yipping intensifies as we get out of the SUV. A bowlegged man in jeans, work boots, and a shearling-lined jean jacket steps out of a single story barn-like building to greet us.

"Hey, Jesse. Long time." He grips Jesse's arm while he shakes his hand.

"Mr. Anderson, good to see you." His smile is genuine and disarms me.

"Haven't seen you since Cody's funeral. Such a fucking tragedy." His eyes flick to me. "Sorry for the cussing."

Funeral?

Not retired. Dead.

My mouth hovers open and I clamp it shut when Jesse glances at me.

Play it cool, Mara. You don't know him well. There's probably a good reason why you don't know more about his brother.

Now my curiosity is piqued even more about Willow. Is she Cody's widow? Is he dating his dead brother's ex? What sort of soap opera is this?

"You must be Dr. Keiley." Mr. Anderson steps forward with his hand extended. "Thanks for coming out to see us. We've known Elizabeth a long time."

I shake his hand while imagining Jesse and I starring in a telenovela set in Colorado. "Thanks for allowing me to come visit you."

"I suppose you want to see the dogs. Let's visit the kennels and then we can get warm inside with coffee and some of Granny's pie. You like pecan?"

Evil people who neglect and abuse dogs don't typically offer you homemade pie. At least this is what I tell myself as we walk through the kennel.

The dogs are excited, but generally in good health. I don't see anything alarming or that raises any warnings. Sure, the kennels could use some updates, but overall, it's above board. Mr. Anderson shows me their storage and grooming areas while we talk about genetics and breeding. I try to gently encourage him to spay and neuter the majority of his dogs while keeping a few to breed. Lines get too inbred and the quality of the dogs suffers, bringing on cancers and joint issues. Satisfied the operation is compliant, I ask about the pie he mentioned when we arrived.

Inside a log house with a large stone fireplace, we sip coffee and eat big slices of pecan pie. A big scoop of ice cream melts on the top of mine. Who cares if it's ten-thirty in the morning? Pie is the best breakfast food there is.

I make some recommendations for a salve for the dogs' pads and offer to bring a mobile unit out a couple of times a year for shots and exams.

Once we are bumping along the unpaved road back to the main highway, I confess to Jesse I imagined a nightmare.

"You've got to give people the benefit of the doubt. Most of us have good intentions, even if we don't know better."

"I've heard horror stories. We took in five dogs and eight cats from a hoarding situation down valley when I first arrived." My eyes well up at the memory. "Those poor innocent beasties."

He covers my hand with his. "You have a kind heart, Mara Keiley."

"I'm a big mush ball." I swipe away a few tears.

"You did good back there. Anderson's not the easiest man to get along with. You had him wrapped around your finger. I bet he'll do right just to keep on your good side."

"Then he's a smart man." I smirk at him and he returns it with a grin of his own. "Let's go celebrate."

He frowns for a second and then recovers. "Can't. I have to be up on the mountain for a meeting in an hour."

"Then how about dinner?"

"Are you asking me out?" A slow smile tugs at his lips

"No. Maybe."

"How about you come over to my place and I'll cook us dinner."

"Okay," I say without pause.

"You like spicy?"

"Depends."

"I'll make my family's green chile stew for you if you can handle a little heat."

He's talking about food, I tell myself.

"I can handle it."

Still about food. Not dirty. Nope.

At least he's not promising to make bratwurst or kielbasa or bangers and mash. I won't be able to keep a straight face if he serves me sausage.

He drops me off at the clinic and gives me his address.

After giving him a quick kiss on the cheek, I hop out of his SUV.

I think I have a date. It might not be a date, but if it is, I'm going to need reinforcements.

I spot the small white sign at the end of a narrow alley and follow the brick path lined with evergreen-filled planter boxes to the front door. Behind the large picture window, lace and silk create a colorful display.

The tinkling of bells hung on the door handle announce my arrival to Aspen's best-kept secret: Cheeks.

Lingerie fills the small space, with everything from demure pink pajamas to a black leather corset.

In my clogs and jeans, I feel out of place in the land of seduction.

"I'll be with you in a second," a female voice calls from the little hall to the left where I assume the dressing rooms are located.

I lift the tag on a teal nightie trimmed in black lace. My eyes bug out at the zeros. "Three hundred dollars? For sleeping?"

"I know, can you believe it? Honestly, most of this stuff ends up on the floor in minutes. I guess that's the point." Sage rounds the corner carrying an armful of bras. "Mara! I didn't realize it was you."

We attempt to hug around the thousands of dollars' worth of lace in her arms.

"What are you doing here?" She drops the pile onto the counter. The ends of her blond hair are pink today and match her loose sweater.

"Shopping?" The word comes out a question.

"Oh, do you have a hot date?" Wiggling her eyebrows, she does a little shimmy dance.

"Maybe?" Why does my voice keep rising at the end of every one-word sentence? I'm buying underwear, not a dungeon costume. My gaze slides over to the leather corset.

Sage follows my focus and then she playfully slaps my arm. "Kinky stuff? Ooh, you have to tell me who."

The roots of my hair blush as my face heats. "No! No, no. No."

At least I don't think so, although Jesse is kind of bossy. My eyes bug out. What if he's into bondage and making me call him Big Daddy?

"I'm more of a cotton and comfort kind of girl, but whatever floats your balloon. No judgment from me." Sage pats my arm.

"Me too." I poke the boning of a lace bodysuit-corset combination. "This looks uncomfortable."

"I totally agree. Lee loves me in one of his shirts." She twirls a pink strand of hair around her finger. "And nothing else."

"Sounds comfortable."

"So what brings you in here? Or who?"

I'm not sure why I'm reluctant to tell her it's Jesse.

"Please tell me it isn't Landon." She whispers his name like it's a swear word.

My gag is involuntary. "God no."

Her exhale comes out in a relieved whoosh of air. "Good. I wouldn't wish him on anyone but my worst enemy. Not that I have enemies."

"You know him?"

Solemnly, she nods her head. "In the biblical sense."

"I'm so sorry."

"You?"

"Thankfully, no. We only went out once."

"He's like a cold virus."

"Why'd you think I was dating him?"

She ducks her head and focuses on the bra she's folding. "It's a small town."

"I'm fodder for gossip?"

"The guys are the worst. Lee and the rugby crew gossip like a bunch of high school girls. And they have a book with rules on who's off limits to date."

"Seriously?"

She nods. "It's supposed to cut down on cross-pollination or something, but I think it's about marking territory."

"What've you heard about me?"

"Mae said Jesse Hayes kissed you in the middle of La Belle Femme."

Of course Mae saw us. At least she didn't bring it up during Taco Tuesday in front of the rest of the girls.

"So, it's true?"

I meet her eyes. "It's a long story, but yes, he kissed me during my so-called date with Landon." I'm still not sure if the kiss was for my benefit or to piss of Landon.

She pauses her folding and her eyes light up. "Tell me all the details."

I fill her in on most of the details, including the way Jesse and I met.

"It's a great love story!"

"I don't know about love."

"Trust me. I've known Jesse for a few years. He's not a player like most of the other guys. Definitely more serious and keeps to himself. When are you seeing him again?"

"Tonight."

Grinning, she snaps her fingers. "I knew it! Okay, let's find you something amazing."

In a few minutes, I'm shoved into a dressing room with an armload of pretty, feminine lingerie.

"Don't worry about the prices. You get the friends and family discount!"

I try on more lace and silk than I've ever worn in my life up until this point. Sage pokes her head through the curtain and gives me her opinion. When she wraps up my purchase, I know I've made the perfect choice.

TWENTY

MARA

SHOWERED, DRESSED, AND as ready as I'll ever be, I drive
to Jesse's house as the sun sets. *I'm not nervous. You're nervous.*
I follow the twist in the road and cross a narrow bridge over
Woody Creek gurgling below. I've been down to the infamous
tavern of the same name before, but never to Jesse's place. My
foot eases off the gas and hovers over the brake as I pass the
first trailers.

Oh my . . .

No.

Mr. High Altitude fantasy man cannot live in a . . .

I spot his number.

He lives in a trailer park.

"Just my luck." I slam my hand against my steering wheel
and end up honking my horn.

Of course he's not perfect. No one is. I'm not perfect. Just
ask my mother.

But a trailer? In a trailer park?

I suppose a trailer in the back woods with old cars rusting
away in the yard might be worse.

Or a cabin in the woods without running water or electricity. Worse.

Living in his parents' basement. Worse.

Frat house. Worse.

Married.

We have a winner.

Living with a wife would be worse than a trailer in the Roaring Fork Valley. Aspen's only a twenty minute drive away. Snowmass even less.

It's not like he's in the backwoods.

These mobile homes probably cost a small fortune.

I listen for the sound of banjos when I make the turn into the spot behind his SUV.

My headlights illuminate the small deck by the front of the trailer.

Only . . .

I lean forward to get a better eyeful of what I'm walking into tonight.

It's not a trailer. Exactly.

The width is a little broader than a single wide, but instead of a flat roof, there's a second story. Warm wood siding covers the entire two story unit.

Home.

There's nothing mobile about it.

A knocking on my window makes me jump.

"Are you going to sit out here all night staring with your mouth open, or do you want to come inside? I can probably slide a sandwich through the window if you'd prefer."

Jesse stands next to my CRV with a grin plastered on his stupidly handsome face. He's wearing jeans and a dark blue thermal that clings to his pecs and arms. Fern jumps up and rests her paws on the door handle, startling me out of my

Jesse ogling.

I manage to close my mouth and swallow before opening my door.

Once I'm out of the car, Fern jumps with all four feet off the ground and spins mid-air.

"Someone's excited to see you," Jesse says, happiness brightening his voice. I hope the someone he means is him.

"I brought her a treat." I hold up the plush duck squeaky toy. "I remember you said she's a duck trolling retriever."

Standing on her hind legs, Fern tries to take her new toy.

Jesse smiles at her and I can see the love he has for his dog. "Fern, don't forget your manners."

She sits down and holds out a paw for a shake. I hold her paw and then give her the duck, which she quickly takes and begins happily squeaking.

"Maybe I should've bought the silent squeaker kind." I grimace at the ear-piercing sounds coming from the toy.

"She'll silence it within hours. Thanks for thinking of her." He gives me a soft smile and does a game show hostess gesture in front of his place. "Welcome."

"This isn't exactly a trailer." I point at the classic version a few yards away on the next lot. "That's a trailer."

"You sound disappointed." He takes the two steps up to the front door in one smooth leap, Fern bounding after him.

"I don't know what to think." Still frozen by my car, I try to absorb his house. It's not exactly a tiny house or something you could pull behind a truck. Nor is it a regular, normal house.

"Shaking up your preconceptions, Doc?" He opens a glass door framed in similar wood to the siding. "Wait until you see the view from my bedroom."

Now I know he's messing with me. "Presumptuous much?"

"It's part of the basic tour." He leans close to my ear as

I pass him to enter the house. "Your virtue is safe with me."

"Sounds like something the wolf would say to Red Riding Hood right before he lures her into the woods."

His deep laugh echoes close behind me. "Woof."

My laughter dies in my chest when I see the glint of lust in his eyes.

"My what full lips you have," I say, softly.

He stalks closer to me. "The better to kiss you with."

I back up until I hit something solid behind me and yelp. When he leans in close like he's going to kiss me, I hold my breath in anticipation.

"Want something to drink?" His dimple flashes.

I blink back at him.

"Cat got your tongue then?" He shakes his head and chuckles. "Don't be so nervous, Doc."

"I'm . . ." I softly clear my throat, "not nervous."

"Why would you be?" He places a quick kiss on my lips before retreating. "Follow me."

Instead, I face the hard object I bumped into and realize it's a narrow console table. It has a slab of wood with bark along the irregular edge. The craftsmanship is beautiful. My fingers brush against the smooth surface of the top.

"You like?" His voice carries through the space beyond the little entry.

"It's gorgeous." I follow the curves of the wood grain with my index finger.

"Thanks. I made it." Pride rings clear in his voice.

"With your bare hands?" I'm stroking his wood. Or wood he's stroked. Either way, I've gone to the pervy side within minutes of entering his house. I touch the table one more time before taking in the rest of the first floor.

My mouth drops open again. "Wow."

"Not what you were expecting?" He smirks at me from the

other side of a large open room with a living room on one end and a kitchen on the far side. Something delicious simmers on the stove. Unfamiliar guitar music softly plays from a Bluetooth speaker.

The only thing I can do is shake my head.

"This might make me sound like a giant nerd, but is this a TARDIS?"

There's no way we're inside a trailer. Dark wood, aged and nicked like it's been hand finished, covers the floor. Two walls are a soft gray. Less outdated basement and more design magazine, pale and distressed paneling decorates the space behind the flat screen. In a corner sits a wood stove next to a worn leather chair that screams curl up here and read a book. Maybe because two overstuffed bookshelves fill the wall nearby.

"Do you want a beer? Fat Tire? Wine? Or I have Woody Creek vodka, if you want something with more of a kick."

I'm too dumbstruck by the room to answer him.

"Sorry, I shouldn't assume you want a drink. Water? Root beer?"

"Sure." I run my hand over the soft wool blanket on the back of the old chesterfield sofa. Faded Navajo rugs and Pendleton blankets add color to the manly space.

He chuckles. "Were you expecting a stained couch held together with duct tape and a beanbag chair?"

Busted. "Maybe. I wasn't expecting this. Did you build this place?"

"I did. With these." He lifts his hands and wiggles his fingers.

"I'm so confused," I whisper, mostly to myself.

"About your drink choices? No pressure."

"Huh? Oh, I'll have a beer." I'm still petting the blanket, wondering if I can sneak it out in my purse and take it home.

He hands me a bottle of Fat Tire. "Do you think you can handle seeing the rest of the house? You can bring the blanket with you if you want."

Embarrassment heats my cheeks. "It's a really nice blanket."

"Come on." Tugging my sleeve, he guides me around the kitchen island with its wood cabinets and island topped with a slab of warm-colored granite. "You?"

"All me." At the back of the house is a staircase leading us up to the top floor.

Windows near the ceiling run the length of the short hall.

"Office, bathroom, guest room," he rattles off words as he backs down the hall.

I peek into darkened rooms through open doors, resisting the temptation to flip on lights and explore.

"You built this place?"

"I can show you the photos if you don't believe me." He pulls me along with him.

"Why here?"

"You mean in a trailer park?" His lips tug upward with a small smile.

I nod.

"My uncle left me his spot and an old single-wide when he died. I was living down valley with two other guys in a one bedroom and jumped on the chance to have my own space. I read up on the bi-laws and figured I could build a custom house on the slab. So I did."

"This place is gorgeous."

"Someday when I buy my own land, I can move the house. Or build another one with the profit I make off of this."

Knowing the cost of real estate around here, he'll make bank.

He steps into the room at the end of the hall. Instead of flipping on the light, he guides me over to a huge window facing south. Blue twilight highlights snowcapped mountains. "Wow."

"Not a bad thing to wake up to, is it?" He grins down at me

and I swear my heart rate quickens.

"No, not at all." I'm sure there's the usual furniture in the space, but all I can focus on is Jesse, the view behind him, and the enormous bed taking up most of the room. I never want to leave.

"Are you hungry?" he asks.

"Starved."

"I made my grandmother's green chile stew."

I'm staring at his mouth forming words. It's mesmerizing.

"Come on." He tugs my hand.

I assume he wants to kiss me, so I launch myself at him.

He's still smiling as he kisses me, sweeping his tongue into my mouth. His hands find their favorite place on my butt.

Running my hand through his waves, I tug his head closer. Tangling my tongue with his, I press my chest against his, soft against hard. Speaking of hard, I feel his length against my stomach. How could I ever think he could have a micro penis? With a content sigh, I kiss the soft skin behind his ear.

The light outside his door highlights the fat, heavy snowflakes tumbling to the ground.

"Was it supposed to snow tonight?" I peer out the window at the thick coating of snow already covering the cars and walkway.

"Why?" he asks from the kitchen where he's washing dishes. I offered and he refused to let me help.

"Because it is and looks like it's coming down hard."

Lord help me for thinking the words coming and hard together in the same room as him.

I feel his warmth behind me at the window. "You're right. You should probably stay the night."

"Wait, what?" I point outside. "It's only a few inches. Nothing I can't handle."

Again, I take something innocent and around him, my mind makes it perverted.

"You've had a couple of drinks. It's not safe." He walks over to me.

"I'm fine."

"Safety first." A stern tone in his voice warns me not to argue with him.

"I think you mean always in control. As in you always want to be in control."

"I can't in good conscience let you drive home. What if you slide off the road and freeze to death? Or get out of the car and go wandering in a blizzard?"

"Why would I get out of the car?"

"Because you're stubborn enough to walk home in a snowstorm."

He has a point, but I won't concede.

Because I am stubborn.

"I grew up driving in the snow and ice. I have my cell phone. I'm a responsible adult."

"You're not leaving." He frowns at me. Something in his eyes shifts and darkens. "I can make you not want to leave."

I step away and he stalks closer. "How?"

The word quivers in the air between us.

A wolfish grin spreads across his full, soft lips. "First, I'm going to ply you with dessert."

"Oh really?" I narrow my eyes. "You think I'll stay for a sugar fix?"

"I have the triple chocolate gelato you like."

I involuntarily moan. "How do you know what kind of ice cream I like?"

He traps me against the counter. "I have my ways."

"Lucky guess? Girls like chocolate."

"Or I peeked in your basket when we ran into each other

at the market."

"Sneaky."

"Do you want it now or later?"

"What comes later?"

"Up to you. I think I have a checkerboard around here some-where. Maybe a backgammon set." His breath warms my neck as he dips his head to kiss my exposed skin.

"Games? You want to play games?"

"Unless you have other suggestions."

If I tilt my hips forward, I'd be able to make contact. Somehow, I resist. I need him to make the first move.

As he trails his nose along my jaw, a soft sigh escapes my mouth. "Sure. Backgammon sounds good."

"Really?" I feel his smile against my skin.

"Sure."

He pulls away enough to stare into my eyes. "I'm not sure I even have checkers."

"Then why did you offer?"

"I was teasing." He nips the corner of my jaw. The gesture feels like a promise of something far more entertaining than board games.

"What, what else did you have in mind?" My voice shakes as I try to keep playing cool.

His fingers tangle in the hair at the nape of my neck and he gently pulls my head back, exposing more of my neck. He trails warm, open mouth kisses along my skin. I try to resist grabbing his shoulders and anchoring him to me.

I last for about ten seconds before I grip his biceps. I've been wanting to touch them forever. They do not disappoint.

Whatever distance and propriety I've been keeping between us vanishes as I press myself against the rest of his body from chest to thigh. Our height difference makes this challenging. Frustrated, I groan and squirm.

He must sense my annoyance, because he lifts me up to his level. My legs dangle for a moment before I wrap them around his hips. He carries me over to the couch and sits so I'm straddling him.

"Better?" he asks against my lips.

"Much." I rest my forearms on his shoulders and weave my fingers into his hair.

For a moment I stare down at him, noticing his long lashes and the little bit of copper in his beard and hair.

His soft hair slips through my fingers as I scratch his scalp.

"Don't stop," he growls and grips my hips, angling me over him.

I never want to stop and that scares me. To distract myself, I release his hair and tilt up his chin to kiss him.

He stretches his neck to meet my mouth before pulling me closer. He growls softly, "You stopped."

After placing my hands back on his hair, he kisses me. Gently sucking my bottom lip into his mouth, he drags his teeth against my skin before slowly releasing it. Soft and sharp blend together into a new sensation. All evening I've been on a slow simmer. His growl and slow, soft kisses combine with my anticipation into a brewing storm beneath my skin.

I'll always remember this kiss. How he purrs in the back of his throat in pleasure when our tongues meet. Or how his hands flex against where he holds me when I pull his hair.

The best kind of déjà vu washes over me.

This is what I've been missing. No other guy kisses me the way he does or makes my skin flame with a single touch. I want to strip off every barrier between us and press my skin against every inch of him.

For the first time in years, I breathe.

He is the oxygen I've been starved for.

Panting, I drag my cheek along his scruff and then nip at his earlobe. His own ragged breath brushes against my neck as his fingers slip beneath my sweater. He slides his hands over my stomach and ribs, resting them below my sexy new bra, barely touching my aching breasts. It's not enough.

"More," I whisper, licking the tender smooth skin behind his ear.

He cups me through the pale rose satin and it's still not enough. I need skin against skin, his rough hands on my smooth curves. With a single index finger, he traces the outline of my nipple through my bra before softly sucking the peaked flesh into his mouth. When he moves to the other breast, his fingers pinch the satin where it's wet from his mouth. Encouraging him, I arch my back.

With each slow, tortuous touch, he makes me burn more for him. Every small movement is a drop of gasoline on an existing fire, sending up a new burst of bright flame.

I wriggle and grind on his lap. Discovering he's hard beneath his jeans empowers me. I do this to him.

"Slow down." He stills my hands where they struggle with his belt buckle.

"I'm not sure I can." Pushing aside his T-shirt, I run my fingers along the ridges of his stomach. I can feel each individual muscle contract with his laughter.

"You started this." I push out my bottom lip in a pout.

He kisses my full bottom lip. "And I intend to finish it."

I moan against his mouth.

He grins while trying to continue the kiss. "Still want to leave?"

I begin to protest but he silences me by flipping me beneath him on the sofa. He settles between my legs, grinding against my heat. The press of the smooth satin against my sensitive, swollen flesh is almost enough to bring on an orgasm. Almost.

When his eyes meet mine, they're full of mischief and

desire. "Didn't think so."

He's going to be the death of me.

Death by orgasm.

I don't know how I could've ever thought he sucked in bed. Or how I could've forgotten how my body responds to him.

"Still want to play games?" He slowly lifts my sweater.

"N-no." My voice falters as he pulls the fabric over my head. In spite of the fire in the wood stove, the air feels cool against my skin. I shiver from the contrast between the way my skin burns for him and the colder air.

Reaching behind his head, he yanks his T-shirt off in the sexiest way to remove an article of clothing ever. He rests his weight on top of me and I melt when his warm skin touches mine. Every nerve ending screams for attention from him. My breasts press against the smooth planes of his chest. We're a study in opposites. Where I'm soft, he's hard. He's all straight lines and angles where I'm round and curvy. He's opposite in almost every way, yet we fit together perfectly.

He shifts and rolls slightly to the side, allowing space for his hands between us.

When he brushes his thumb across my nipple, my back arches. I'm greedy for his touch. I reach behind my back to unclasp my bra.

"Uh, uh," he chastises me. "My job."

I love it when he takes control. He flicks open the clasp and drags the straps over my shoulders. Before he removes it entirely, he drags his nose across the fullness above each cup, kissing my nipples through the rose satin. He runs his tongue along the peak and blows warm air on the wet lace.

"More," I beg shamelessly. I'm about two seconds from ripping out of my remaining clothes like the Hulk when he's angry.

He nips my left breast with his teeth, not painfully but sharp enough to let me know he's in charge. I squirm and twist beneath him. He stills me with a hand on my hip as he finally removes my bra.

At this pace, we're going to need to be snowed in for days. I'm not complaining.

While he nuzzles and kisses my breasts, I stroke my hands over his shoulders and down his back. His muscles shift and contract under my touch. He shouldn't be allowed to wear shirts. I wonder if he goes shirtless in the summer when he's working on projects. I imagine his chest and back in the sun, a slight sheen of sweat on his skin as he swings a hammer or uses power tools to build things. Sweet heavens, I don't think I can survive summer Jesse.

He squeezes one breast as he kisses and sucks the nipple on the other. I admire his multi-tasking abilities. His other hand moves down my stomach.

"Please, yes."

Until this moment, I've never understood how a person can mewl like a kitten. My soft and plaintive begging holds a familiar feline desperation. I really might die if he keeps denying me.

He rests his palm against my heat and I'm about to come undone. He's barely applying pressure. To encourage him, I lift my hips and moan as pleasure pulses beneath his touch.

His mouth against my breast, one hand squeezing the other. Pressing his palm against my most sensitive spot, he releases my nipple. I feel his cheeks lift. He's smiling while I'm dying. "We could *still* play checkers."

TWENTY-ONE

JESSE

IF IT WEREN'T snowing outside, I still would've asked her to stay the night.

Even Mother Nature is on my side.

I can't stop teasing her. I want to hear her tell me how much she wants me.

I need her to say the words.

We've been dancing around each other for weeks.

Seeing her naked, or almost naked at the hotel has been torturing me ever since. I got a glimpse, but didn't want to stare. For the past month, I've spent more time jerking off than I have since junior high after discovering Wyatt's stash of porn.

I've imagined her breasts from the glimpse in the pool, but my brain didn't do them justice.

She's perfect.

Soft curvy, perfection.

Now that I have her alone without interruptions, I want to take my time with her, savor her, and drive her crazy from pleasure.

I have a plan.

And it doesn't involve board games.

I pop open the button on her jeans and slide down the zipper.

With the back of my fingers, I brush against lace and heat, fighting back a moan of pleasure.

She tightens her grip on my shoulders.

I lean away to remove her pants and she lifts her hips to help. My erection presses against my fly and I adjust it to relieve some of the pressure. Her eyes follow my movement and she licks her lips. This moment is more than I ever imagined and I've had years of practice.

Tugging off her jeans, I leave her in only a pair of pink underwear. They're simple with a little lace along the edge and that makes them even sexier. I don't need bows and fancy shit. Most men don't. We'll take naked over costumes almost every time. The rest of it is wrapping on the present. We want to rip it off to get to the good stuff.

"You're staring." Her hand cups my cheek.

"Busted. Don't care. You're beautiful." No other woman compares to Mara.

"You've seen me naked before."

"Doesn't count. You weren't naked for me." I want to ask her to be mine.

Her eyes crinkle with her smile. "You're still wearing pants. Can I help you with those?"

She runs her hand along my obvious erection. The press of the zipper is almost painful against my skin, and I sigh in relief when she undoes my fly. I roll over and pike above her, giving her room to shove the denim off my hips. Our feet and legs tangle together as we try to remove my pants from our horizontal position.

"This is a terrible idea." I brace myself and lift off the couch. Once I'm standing, I kick off my jeans.

She looks beautiful sprawled topless on my couch. Her blond curls create a bright halo around her head. Every curve and peak is on display for me. I drop to my knees in front of her.

Comprehension flashes in her eyes when I shift her legs to either side of my shoulders. Slowly, I slip her underwear off and then drop it on the pile of her clothes. Our eyes meet again and I see hesitation in hers. As I press soft kisses along her inner thigh, I will her to understand how much I desire her and want to do this. I brush my lips over where she wants me most and kiss the tender flesh on her other leg.

Working my way up to her hip, I drag my chin against her skin alternating between soft kisses and the roughness from my beard. Each time she lifts her hips, wanting more, I retreat. When she groans, I smile and nip her skin right above the small patch of soft curls.

"Jesse." A sharp tug of her fingers in my hair warns me her patience is running out.

If she only knew.

I finally relent from the teasing and run my tongue gently along her sensitive skin. This elicits a gasp of relief and pleasure I've been fantasizing about for what feels like forever.

It's taking every scrap of willpower for me not to plunge into her. But I want . . . no, I need this to be good for her. We'll never get another first time and I want to make sure she never forgets tonight.

Using my tongue and fingers, I focus on bringing her to the edge. She quivers and clenches as she gets closer to coming. I ease back, slowing my pace to intensify her pleasure. Slipping another finger inside her, I gently suck with my mouth. Keeping up the same pace and pressure until a soft gasp falls from her lips. I swear she whispers my name and I nearly lose my mind. It's the sexiest sound I've ever heard.

"I'm close, please, so close." She emphasizes her pleas by raising her hips and tightening her hold on my hair. "Jesse."

I keep up the same pace and pressure, and pinch her nipple

with a gentle squeeze. The surprise jolt of pain combines with the soft strokes of my tongue to send her into bliss.

Lifting my eyes, I watch her come apart as she clenches around my fingers. There's nothing more beautiful than a woman letting go in pleasure. Fucking insane how much I want her right now. I guide her down from her orgasm with soft kisses, avoiding her most sensitive spot.

She opens her eyes and stares at me with her lips slightly parted.

"Hi." I kiss her hip and she jolts, still sensitive from her orgasm.

"How could I ever think you were bad at sex?" Her words are slightly slurred and her eyes aren't focused.

"I don't know." Softly kissing a trail over her stomach, I rest my head on her stomach. "Why would you think that?"

"Because I couldn't remember."

I kiss the underside of her left breast. "Because nothing happened."

"But I didn't know that." She frowns and I lean forward to kiss it away.

"Stop torturing yourself." I place soft kisses along her jaw. "Nothing horrible happened. We didn't have sex. I want you fully aware when I'm having sex with you."

She hums and runs her fingers through my hair. "Speaking of having sex . . ."

"Yes?" My cock swells as I think about being inside of her.

She hooks a finger in my boxers and brings me closer. I still when she dips her hand beneath the fabric to grip me.

A wicked grin settles over her mouth. "Yes."

I brush a curl from her forehead, holding my breath as she licks her lips. Her tongue makes contact first, swirling around the head before she opens her mouth to place a soft kiss to the tip. Never breaking eye contact, she licks and kisses down the length before opening her mouth. I exhale long and slow to keep from thrusting as she wraps her lips around me, covering the rest of my length with her hand.

A slew of silent curses form and leave my lips as I watch her. I'm not sure it's possible, but every moment she becomes sexier, more beautiful, and impossible to resist. Standing above her while she sits on the couch creates the perfect angle. I rest my hand on her head, not to direct her, but to balance myself as pulses of intense pleasure begin firing along the base of my spine. I could easily come in her mouth, but that's not what I want. Not for our first time. I softly brush my finger along the side of her face.

She pauses and makes eye contact. Still griping my base, she slides her mouth off and gives me a questioning smile. Fuck. The look in her eyes right now kills me.

"You're amazing, but all I can think of is being inside of you right now."

She places one more soft kiss to the tip and removes her hand.

"I'll be right back." I race upstairs to grab a condom and return in record time, my erection bouncing like a conductor's baton.

I pick her up and settle her over my lap as I sit down. All night I've kept the pace slow, but now I feel frenzied, unable to get close enough. She helps with the condom and sits up on her knees, taking me in her hand again, and brushing the head of my cock against her wetness. I fight the urge to rush the moment, stilling my hips when all I want to do is thrust. Slowly she slides down my length until our hips meet. Her tight warmth engulfs every inch of me. The sensation overwhelms me and I close my eyes, inhaling slowly through my nose. I kiss her deeply, brushing her tongue with mine. Sucking on her bottom lip, I bite down playfully.

When she scrapes her nails along my scalp, I moan into her mouth.

My hands settle on her hips and I gently rock her above me. I need more.

I flip us over and plunge into her with strong, deep thrusts.

Closing my eyes, I focus on the feeling of her body responding to mine. Her soft gasps, the way her hips arch off the couch to meet mine, the way her skin flushes across her chest—I memorize them all. Pressure begins building and I know I'm not going to last much longer. I want to feel her come around me. I press my thumb against her lips and she opens for me, sucking on the tip. I remove my thumb and kiss her again, rubbing small circles with my thumb right above where our bodies are joined. The pressure on her clit sends her into another orgasm and she pulses around me. My thrusts become erratic as my orgasm slams into me.

Everything shrinks to a pinpoint. My reality begins and ends with her. The world contains only us. And it's enough.

I rest my head against her shoulder, trying to calm my racing pulse and catch my breath. Her own chest rapidly rises and falls beneath my own as she strokes her hands down my back.

Aware I'm probably crushing her beneath me, I lift myself up on my elbows and give her a kiss.

"Take me upstairs." Her hesitation about staying from earlier has disappeared completely.

"Or lose you forever?" I finish the quote.

Her eyes widen. "You remember?"

I nod.

Standing, I pull her to her feet. "I need to let her out one more time for the night before we go to bed."

"Shit!" Mara's eyes widen and she covers her mouth.

"What's wrong?" My post-sex bubble pops with her freak out.

"Tapper. He's stuck inside. I didn't think I'd be gone all night."

I glance at the clock on the stove. "It's only nine. Can you call someone?"

Chewing her bottom lip, she stares out the window at the heavy falling snow.

"What about Elizabeth? She lives on the property, doesn't she?"

"I don't want to bother her."

I gently brush one of her curls behind her ear. "You're not driving up to the ranch in this, so you either have to clean up a mess tomorrow or bug your boss now. Better sooner than later."

Still gloriously naked, she finds her phone to make the call, sounding relieved when Elizabeth answers.

I pull on my boxers and call upstairs to Fern where she's put herself to bed in my room. Outside, I gauge the new snowfall to be about four inches already. At this rate we'll get a foot of fresh powder overnight. Great for skiing, but could lead to possible avalanches. I'll have to leave early in the morning to get up to the mountain.

Fern runs back inside, covered in white and looking like an Arctic wolf. Still wearing only my boxers, I shiver against the cold.

Mara's slipped on my shirt instead of her own. I like it. She leans down to brush the snow off of Fern's coat, giving her a scratch behind the ears and a kiss to the top of her head. Fern wags her tail.

"I'm all yours," Mara says with a smile.

If only she meant it beyond tonight.

"Good. I plan to keep you." I stalk toward her. "Still want

to play checkers?"

"No, I think we should go to bed." She turns down the hall.

"I like the way you think." Scooping her up in my arms, I carry a giggling Mara upstairs.

TWENTY-TWO

JESSE

MY MIND IS still on last night when I hit the locker room to change after my shift. After we went upstairs, we spent hours exploring each other's bodies. Skipping seven hours of sleep was worth every moment with her. I paid for it this morning, but that's why we have endless coffee in the patrol shacks.

Fern jumps down from her chair by the stove and stretches, her tail swishing behind her.

"Ready to go home?"

She spins in a circle. I scratch her butt.

"I'll take that as a yes."

I text Mara as I walk out the door, letting her know I'm done for the day.

Outside, the number of skiers and boarders has thinned. Even though I'm officially off duty, I'm still working until I get to base village and walk off the mountain for the day.

Overall, it's been a slow day, so I let Fern run between my skis as we descend the blue runs from the shack at the top of Big Burn. We haven't had fresh powder in a week, and the runs are packed down and a little slushy from today's strong sun.

From uphill I hear a group of rowdy voices and check over

my shoulder to see a bunch of boarders in crazy hats speeding down the intermediate run. They're going too fast to maintain control in the less than ideal conditions. I guide Fern and I over to the tree line to avoid them. After I stop, she runs a few feet beyond me before she realizes I'm not beside her.

At the sound of my whistle, she stops and turns to come back to me, a happy smile on her face as she pants.

A flash of color flies past me, heading directly for Fern. Someone screams and there's a yelp of pain. Everything happens too fast for my eyes to process. I blink and look at the boarder lying on the snow in front of me. I'm still standing in the same spot. He missed me by some miracle.

Where's Fern?

Panicked, I search the area for her brown fur and smiling face. I call out her name, listening for a response.

"Fern!"

I hear a quiet whimper closer to the trees.

"Why is there a dog on a ski run?" the guy sits up, slurring his words. "Or was that a wolf?"

"If she's hurt—" I don't finish the thought as I start to see red. I snap out of my skis and rush to the trees. Fern lifts her head and whines.

I reach her and see blood on the snow near her hind leg.

"You hurt my dog, asshole." I reach for my radio, but realize I'm not wearing my uniform. "Someone call ski patrol!"

A few skiers have stopped behind me. "We saw what happened if you need to file a report," an older woman offers.

I nod, but my focus is on Fern. "Can you stand, girl?"

She's on her side and I can't tell where the blood is coming from.

With effort, she pushes up on her front legs, but she doesn't put any weight on her back left leg. In the deep snow, she can't seem to get her balance to get up. I move closer and rest my hand on her neck. "It's going to be okay. It's going to be fine. You're okay."

I'm not sure who I'm reassuring, her or me.

I crouch next to her and slide my hands underneath her belly. "Let's get you out of here." I'm using my ski patrol voice, faking a calmness I don't feel.

Once she's in my arms, I can see the gash on her leg. It's deep and about four inches long.

My stomach rises into my throat and my lunch threatens a return. "You fucking asshole." I'm torn between kicking the shit out of him and helping Fern.

I notice the boarder's friends have left him behind, but a couple skiers stand around him, making sure he doesn't leave. His eyes flick to Fern and me, then down at his board.

Carefully I lay Fern on the packed snow. I need to wrap the cut before I get her down the mountain. She's going to need stitches and probably an X-ray to make sure nothing's broken.

I kneel over her and try to open my pack, but my hands are shaking.

A woman hands me a fleece neck warmer. "Here, use this."

I press it against Fern's leg and she whimpers again. "Thank you."

"Want me to beat him up for you?" she offers.

I glance over my shoulder at her. She has short silver hair and can't be under fifty or much over five feet tall. Her suggestion makes me smile. I take my first deep breath in minutes. "Think you can take him?"

"I'd give it my best shot. I go to kickboxing classes three times a week. I've always wanted to kick someone's ass and he's the perfect candidate. I can't stand people who are reckless on the mountain and ruin it for everyone else. Bunch of punks and entitled brats."

Her spunky spirit reminds me of my grandmother, Inez,

who never suffered any fools or disrespect.

I keep pressure on Fern's leg for another minute. Deep red stains the pink fleece.

"I need to get her off the mountain." Opening my pack, I pull out the first aid kit. I use tape and gauze to wrap the wound.

As I'm finishing up, Abe arrives with the toboggan. "We got a report of a collision and injury. Who's hurt?"

"Fern."

"Someone crashed into Fern?"

"Who has a dog on a ski slope?" the culprit asks again and I notice a pronounced scent of beer on his breath.

"She's a ski patrol dog, you—" Abe's hand on my chest stops me.

"You take care of Fern, we'll handle the incident report. Do you need the sled?"

I nod. With his help, we get her settled in the sled and wrap the blanket around her. She tries to lick the bandage before settling on her side.

"Go on." Abe tucks my poles next to Fern in the toboggan.

The rest of the way down the mountain is a blur. When I get to base, I leave the sled by the lift and carry Fern toward the lot.

I stand with Fern in my arms while I try to figure out what to do next. We took the shuttle this morning, so I don't have my car. A local taxi pulls up to the curb, and a familiar face appears in the window.

"Heard you need an emergency run to the hospital," Darren says as he jumps out to open the back door for us. He's a fixture around town and has driven my drunk ass home more times than I can count. In the rugby club, we joke he's our transportation officer.

"How?"

"I listen to the ski patrol channel." He doesn't even sound guilty.

I think he means he's eavesdropping, but I ignore the security breach.

"Can you take us to Hawks Creek?" I shuffle myself and Fern into the backseat, careful not to hit her leg.

I'm reluctant to look at the speedometer as he flies around corners on the way to the ranch. I spend the short ride petting Fern's head and keeping her calm with soft words.

Darren starts honking as we pull down the private road to the clinic.

Mara and a few women I don't recognize rush out of the building to meet us.

I don't think we've come to a full stop when she opens the door and pokes her head in. "Abe called ahead. We've got her. Everything's going to be okay. Do you want me to take her? Or can you manage?"

Her words fly out rapid fire and I respond by exiting the car, Fern in my arms.

Mara pets her neck and places a kiss on the top of Fern's head. "Sweet girl. You're going to be okay."

I suspect the last sentence is more for me. We follow her into the exam room and I lay Fern on the table. Blood has soaked through the bandage.

"You should sit down." Mara presses against my chest, guiding me to a chair.

"I'm fine."

"You look pale and I don't need you fainting. I'm good with stitches, but I've never had to sew up a human before. You pass out and split your head open, I can't promise you won't end up looking like Frankenstein."

As the adrenaline leaves my body, her words get tinny and the room feels hot. I put my head between my knees.

Mara runs her fingers through my hair once before she attends to Fern. "When was the last time she ate?"

"Around five thirty this morning before work," I speak to the floor.

"Good. We won't have to wait to sedate her if her stomach is empty." Her voice is soft as she orders an X-ray and she explains to me each of her actions. "We'll be right back. Stay where you're at. I'll get someone to bring you water and crackers."

I lift my head as she and a vet tech carry Fern out of the room. In the quiet of the clinic, I can hear Fern's whimpers. Hearing her in pain slays me. I've never felt more helpless.

A few moments later, I'm feeling better. More embarrassed than anything, I poke my head out the door. Elizabeth walks down the hall with a large glass of water and a sleeve of saltines.

"Heard you passed out over a little blood." She doesn't temper her grin.

"Don't tell anyone or you'll ruin my tough guy reputation." I take the glass of water from her and gulp down half of it.

"Your secret's safe with me." She offers me a cracker. "When someone we love is hurt, we tend to feel uncertain and helpless."

"Is she going to be okay?"

"Fern's going to be fine. Nothing's broken. Mara's stitching her up. She'll have the cone of shame and a temporary bald spot, but otherwise, she's all good."

"I wonder if ski patrol offers workman's comp for dogs?"

"If she needs a doctor's note, Mara will write her one." Elizabeth squeezes my forearm.

"I owe you a thank you." My mouth dry, I roll my lips together as nerves and panic from earlier begin to fade.

"Me?" She blinks at me. "I only brought you crackers."

"I meant for Mara. Thanks for hiring her."

She assesses me coolly.

"What?" My voice cracks like I'm fourteen again.

"I didn't realize I was playing matchmaker."

I shift my gaze to the wall.

"Are you telling me Jesse Hayes is smitten?"

"I wouldn't use that word." I feel the back of my neck warm.

She continues to study me. "My word. You are."

"Please stop talking." I feel like I'm back in high school and my mother is trying to figure out if I have a girlfriend and encouraging my dad to have "the talk" with me. I stare at the ceiling and blow out a breath.

"Okay, I won't say anything more if you make me a promise."

I cut my eyes over to her and wait for her to continue.

"Don't mess this up. If your intentions are honorable, you have my blessing. But if you screw her over and she quits, I'm going to hunt you down. Finding a good vet who is willing to work for almost nothing and put up with the craziness of the ranch is worth jail time."

Whoa.

I meet her eyes and give her a small smile. "I never want to find out what you would do. You have my word."

"Good. Eat some more crackers. Mara will come find you when she's done."

"Yes, ma'am."

She pats my shoulder on her way out the door. I do as I'm told and munch on crackers while I wait for Mara to finish. I know Mara will take care of my girl.

It's the longest forty minutes of my life. I read all the posters in the room, including the one about intestinal worms. I open the jar of dog biscuits and sniff. They smell almost identical to the saltines I've been eating. Wyatt dared me and Cody to eat Milk-Bones when we were kids. I wonder if these taste similar.

I have my hand in the jar when the door opens again.

"Still hungry after the crackers?" Mara carries Fern into the room.

My sweet girl wags her tail when she spots me. After Mara sets her on the floor, Fern's steps are hesitant and she doesn't put her full weight on her back leg. This doesn't stop her from taking a few steps in my direction. I close the distance and crouch in front of her, gently wrapping my arms around her and burying my face in her fur. Always the one to comfort me, she nuzzles me with her nose before licking my damp cheek.

"Sorry we took so long. I wanted to stay with her until she was awake enough to stand." Mara apologizes unnecessarily.

"Never apologize for caring." I run a hand down Fern's back.

From her hip down, Fern's shaved in a five inch patch. The bare skin has a jagged line of angry black stitches. Around her neck she sports a padded cone of shame to prevent her from licking or chewing on the wound.

I swipe the back of my hand across my eyes. When I speak, I have to clear my throat to get the words out. "She's going to be okay?"

A wave of relief knocks me over. I land on the floor and Fern climbs into my lap. Kissing the top of her head, I inhale her familiar scent. "I was so afraid on the mountain when I saw the blood.

"She's going to be fine. I swear." Mara speaks softly. "You're lucky the cut didn't go too deep into the muscle. Stitches can come out in ten days and she'll heal in a few weeks."

I lift my tear-stained face to see her. "We'll never talk about me crying in public, right?"

Her smile crinkles her watery eyes as she sits on the ground next to me. "Who's crying? I'm not crying."

"No one is crying." I pull her into a half hug, careful not to jostle Fern. "Thank you."

"No need for thank you. We're even." Snuggling into me, she presses a kiss above my heart.

I lean into her touch. "Life's not about checks and balances."

She laughs against my chest. "Then I guess I won't mention you eating dog biscuits either."

I join her with a soft laugh. "I didn't eat them. I only sniffed them."

Fern barks, letting us know if anyone should have a biscuit, it's her.

"See? She's not suffering."

I scratch behind Fern's ear in the softest spot of fur.

Mara bends over to pet her side. "She's not going to be able to go up on the mountain with you until her leg heals."

"I figured. I think she'll have to sit out the rest of the season."

"If you want, she can hang out with Tapper while you work."

"You think they'll get along?"

"Tapper is everyone's best friend. He'd be thrilled to have a canine buddy instead of spending all day with two bitter cats."

I realize I've never seen her place. Or met her pets. "Can I meet them?"

She gives me a shy smile. "Are you asking to come upstairs?"

"I am. I want to know you, Mara."

Her cheeks pink as she gives me a soft smile. "You might change your mind after you meet Fred and George."

"They can't be that bad."

"Do you remember Waldorf and Statler from the Muppets?"

"The two old guys in the theater?"

"Imagine them, only with claws and an appetite for destruction. Especially George. He'll either try to smother you while you sleep or use your shoe as a litter box."

"I'll sleep with one eye open then." I think I invited myself for a sleepover.

"I can make up a bed for Fern where she can rest. Let me tell Elizabeth I'm leaving for the day. Can you give me ten minutes to hide anything embarrassing?"

"Now why would I give you a head start? I'm serious when I say I want to know you. I mean all of you. The good, the beautiful, the weird. Let me in." I stoop to kiss her.

"But my giant granny panties are hanging all over the living room."

I freeze. "Maybe we should have some secrets . . . you know, keep the mystery and excitement alive."

"Why are men so freaked out by full coverage underwear?" She snickers against my mouth.

I've been played.

TWENTY-THREE

MARA

AFTER DOING A sweep of my apartment for anything embarrassing, I bring Tapper downstairs for the introduction. If you didn't know he's missing a foot, you wouldn't notice at first. He has a slight wobble to his walk and on hard surfaces he can sound a little bit like a pirate with a peg leg, but otherwise he's a regular dog.

He and Fern instantly go through first and last name introductions. After a few minutes together outside, we decide to bring Fern upstairs.

"That was quick," I say.

"Kind of like us. One minute they're strangers, the next they're sniffing each other's butts. Or the human equivalent, which I assume is kissing."

I'm walking ahead of him up the stairs. "Do not sniff my butt."

"Can I pinch it instead?"

I cast a look over my shoulder. "Since when do you ask permission?"

He smirks and a familiar wicked gleam flashes in his eyes right before he gives my cheek a little squeeze. I jump and race up the stairs. He follows more slowly with Fern in his arms. Tapper makes sure everyone is accounted for before he hops behind Jesse.

Upstairs Fred and George are less welcoming. Fred's a blur of orange as he races out of the room to hide in my closet. George hisses and arches his back from his current location on top of the fridge. I step between he and Jesse to make sure George doesn't launch himself in an aerial attack.

"Stop your nonsense. He's a guest," I chastise while picking him up. George continues to caterwaul at Jesse from his position in my arms.

Poor Jesse holds up his arms and backs away. Fern stays behind him because she's a smart girl.

I set George on the floor. He hisses, arches his back and dances sideways closer to my guests. I'm about to suggest we go to Jesse's house, when Tapper body slams the cat. George isn't expecting it, so he goes flying across the space, scrambling to get back on his feet.

Tapper barks and growls at George until he skulks away down the hall. Right before he disappears into my room, he stares into my eyes. It's a warning. I don't know when or how, but he will seek his revenge.

Tapper chases after him and George does a perfect vertical jump in surprise.

Jesse laughs and Fern barks, but she doesn't follow Tapper. The poor girl has survived one attack already today.

"Guess I know who's the sheriff around here."

"George's an asshole. He'll seek his revenge for Tapper embarrassing him. You might want to leave your shoes outside."

I'm serious, but Jesse continues chuckling.

"Come here." He holds open his arms and waits for me to step into them.

I accept his hug.

"Thank you," he murmurs into my hair, placing a kiss on the crown of my head.

"For?"

"Fixing Fern, having crazy cats, being you." He tilts my chin up with his index finger before cupping my cheek.

"You might not thank me for George once you get to know him." I kiss his lips to distract him from asking why.

I show Fern to one of Tapper's beds I've dragged to the corner. She lies on her non-injured side and rests her head on her front paws.

"Do you think she's okay?" Jesse asks from behind me. He kneels on the ground to pet her.

"She's going to be out of it because of the drugs, and probably extra sleepy, but yes, she's okay. The best thing for her to do is sleep."

I think about locking the cats in the closet so they don't bother her.

Jesse stands and his eyes darken. "I don't know how to thank you."

His expression tells me he's thinking of several ways to show his gratitude and they're probably going to involve being naked. He steps into my space.

"You've said thanks. I'm happy I could be the one to help her. I adore Fern."

"Thank you." His lips brush mine. "Thank you."

He takes another step and I'm forced to take one back. "You're welcome."

"You're incredible." We take another step backward. "Sexy, adorable, smart, and beautiful."

Standing on my toes, I attempt to kiss him, but I only manage to graze his lips.

He's slowly walking me backward down my hall. "I want to know all of you."

"I hope you want to start with naked me. She's a lot of fun." I bump into the doorjamb but it doesn't stop me. I feel my way to the bed and pull him down on top of me.

He braces himself on his forearms above me. "Oh really?"

I nod and unbutton his jeans.

The next few minutes are a blur of stripping off each other's clothes until we're all warm skin and greedy hands.

He kisses his way down my chest to my navel. I love the direction this is going and happily encourage him with my hands in his hair.

"Patience," he whispers with his lips pressed against my hips.

"Life's short and we only have a limited amount of time before George begins his revenge."

I feel more than hear his laughter as he kisses between my legs.

"This is the only pussy I care about." He licks me and I arch off the bed.

He did not just say that.

I *knew* he was a dirty talker.

"George doesn't have the nuclear codes. We'll be fine."

Jesse draws my attention back to him by nipping my inner thigh. I feel his smile on my skin.

His magical tongue and long fingers get down to the business of making me forget everything but the sensation of his touch. In minutes, I don't know my own name. I'm ninety-seven percent sure I'm moaning and writhing like a woman possessed.

"I love watching you come," he says, softly kissing the corner of mouth.

As I float down from my orgasm, I open my eyes to see his self-satisfied grin.

It's the first time he's used the words I and love and you in a sentence together. I need a moment.

He didn't declare his love for me, but this happy bubble

around us right now feels like falling in love.

I wonder if he feels it, too.

Gripping him, I brush his tip along my slick skin. His eyes close and he hums in pleasure.

He's handsome in any situation, but never more so when he's barely holding on to his control.

"Condoms in the nightstand." I point to the side of the bed where a fresh box was recently tucked inside it.

"I like that you planned for this." He kisses me quickly and reaches across to the drawer.

"Once I figured out you don't suck in bed, I decided we need to have sex as often as possible."

He freezes. "For two years you thought I was terrible in bed?"

I nod and resist telling him my micro-penis theory. I'm holding the evidence to the contrary in my hand, unable to close my fingers around him.

He scoffs. "Let me remind you how not terrible I am."

He does.

Oh boy, does he.

As we lie tangled together, recovering from our orgasms, he brushes his fingers along my back. "You really don't remember what happened that night?"

I snuggle closer to him. "Vague flashes. We went dancing."

"Want me to tell you?"

"Is it awful and embarrassing?" I duck my face into his side.

"Not at all." He kisses the top of my head. "At least not for me."

"Fine. Let's get it over with." Resting my chin on his chest, I stare up at him.

"I'll start at the beginning."

"Be sure you don't leave out a single detail." I lace my words with sarcasm.

"You're adorable."

TWENTY-FOUR

Two Years Ago

JESSE

MARA INSISTS SHE can make me dance and begs me to take her to a club. I'm up for the challenge, so I bring her to Escobar's, a tiny slice of a place with an even smaller dance floor. I'm betting it'll be too crowded to do any actual dancing.

Undeterred, she drags me by the hand into the fray of bodies. I'm so far out of my comfort zone.

"Come on, you're as stiff as a corpse." She wiggles my arms with her hands. "Show me your moves." Pressing herself closer to me, she begins to move, undulating her hips and rubbing her chest against mine.

I grip her hips and growl low in her ear, "I don't dance."

"Fine, stand there. Be the pole. I'll dance around you." She turns around and begins to grind her ass against me.

This woman is going to kill me. She knocks down every wall I've put up and she doesn't even know she's doing it.

I wrap an arm around her waist and dip my head closer to repeat her words from earlier. "I thought you said you weren't a stripper."

"Doesn't mean I don't have moves."

To prove her point, she drapes an arm behind my neck and holds my hand right below her breast. We're connected back to front. There's not enough room between us to slide a piece of paper.

As we move together, I fight getting hard. It's as impossible as resisting her charms.

To save a few scraps of my control, I spin her in my arms to face me. My hands go to her hips and my mouth finds hers.

I couldn't give a fuck who's watching us as we kiss. She wraps a leg around my thigh and grinds against the hard muscles.

Waving the white flag, I give in and move with her. In no sense is this dancing. More like vertical foreplay.

God, I want her.

Suddenly, I have the urge to pull her hair and tip her neck back . . . so I do. I suck on the soft spot behind her ear and feel her shiver in my arms despite the overcrowded and heated space.

A table of women near us open bottles of prosecco and shake them, spraying the crowd.

Great. I love smelling like sweet wine.

Mara slips on the wet floor and tips forward. If I weren't standing behind her, she'd probably face plant. In retrospect, the club was a mistake. She's gone from fun tipsy to probably going to vomit. She's sexy and beautiful, but drunk, which means we're not having sex tonight.

I'm disappointed, but I'll still make sure she gets home safely. It's the right thing to do.

After the prosecco shower, I've had enough fun. I think Mara has too. Her cheeks are permanently flushed and her eyes are glassy.

"Come on, Cinderella. Let's get you back home before one of us turns into a giant squash."

She's giggling and writhing in my arms. Every time she

laughs, her hips brush against the raging hard-on I've been sporting since she made me slow dance with her. The whole evening has been slow burning torture.

I lead us out of the bar and find out where she's staying. Luckily, the condo she's renting is only a few blocks away. An easy walk if we were both sober. An idea pops into my head. I lean forward while bending my knees.

"You look like you're playing football or about to poop on a public toilet."

I chuckle at her random thought process. "Neither. I thought of something. Hop on."

"On what?"

"I'll give you a piggyback ride home."

She stands there blinking at me.

"Come on. I promise not to bounce you too much."

With a cautious expression on her face, she steps behind me. Her arms wind around my neck and I wrap my hands around her thighs. "Ready?"

"Giddy up." She giggles.

Carrying her is easy, but she keeps giggling. When she giggles, she wiggles and presses her chest against my back.

This evening is a study in torture and masochism.

We arrive outside her complex and I gently set her back on her feet.

"You've ruined me for walking."

I wish she said those words for other reasons.

We must come to the same conclusion, because she blushes and fumbles her keys.

Once she manages to pick up her keys from the ground, I take over opening the door to the condo.

"Which one's your room?" I ask in the living area.

She points behind herself. "You want to see it?"

Yes, because I'm a masochist.

"No, that's okay. I can wait here while you shower."

"You're sticky, too." Her shy smile kills me. "We can shower together."

She wobbles on her heels and I steady her. "How about I wait right outside?"

Her full bottom lip gets fuller as she pouts. "You're going to be a gentleman, aren't you?"

"If that means I'm not going to take advantage of a drunk woman, then I guess so." I want to stop talking and kick myself.

The evening started with a plan. Drink. Find a woman. Have sex. Forget myself and my life for a few hours. I thought I had everything in place when Mara fell into my arms. She made me laugh and smile more in a few hours than I have in months. I even forgot to be angry at the world and Cody with her around. Maybe that's why I grew a conscience tonight. I imagine she's incredible in bed if her kisses are anything to go by. She's more than interested and willing.

It kills me I know I'm going to wake up tomorrow without having had sex with her.

It would be so easy to give in and say yes to her.

Why can't I find my morals tomorrow?

A thump and a squeal from the bathroom snap me into action. Rushing down the hall, I find the door open.

Mara's managed to get the shower started, but she forgot the part about taking off her clothes before getting into it.

She waves at me with a happy smile. "My clothes are sticky and smell like prosecco. I thought it would be a good idea to rinse them off, too."

I shake my head and lean a hip against the counter. "I can see the logic, but won't you ruin your dress?"

Smiling, she shrugs. "Not my dress. Sofie will probably kill me, but at least it won't smell like a bridal shower gone wild."

"Why did you scream?" I scan her for injury.

"The water was too cold."

Once I'm certain she'll manage the shower on her own, I should leave, but I don't. Hopping up on the counter, I listen as she rambles. There's no point in trying to follow her thoughts. I zone out until I hear the wet slap of fabric hitting the floor of the shower.

I slide my eyes to the side to confirm she's now topless and about three seconds from naked. My self-control hangs by four thin threads. I drop down from the counter and then go in search of something dry for her to wear. On the top of her suitcase I find a tank and shorts. Without looking at the shower at all, I carry them into the bathroom and leave them on the counter for her.

"I'll wait for you in the other room." I back away, keeping my eyes on my boots and closing the door behind me.

While she finishes, I search the kitchen for a glass. I find one, fill it with water, and set it on her nightstand.

I swear I'll leave as soon as she gets into bed.

The bathroom door swings open and a very pink, clean Mara walks out. The tank and shorts cover only as much as a bathing suit would. Without a bra, her breasts are clearly outlined. Her nipples peak in the cool air of the room. She's beautiful and all round curves.

My resolve weakens.

Clearing my throat, I point to the glass. "I didn't know if you have any ibuprofen, but I brought you some water. You should hydrate. The altitude."

I'm trying not to ogle her as she walks closer to where I sit on the bed. I stand.

"Stay with me?" she asks. With her fresh, makeup-free face she's even more gorgeous. She also looks young and innocent.

My resolve returns.

"I'll stay until your friends return. Come on, get into bed."

"Join me?" She slips underneath the duvet.

Her sleepy eyes can barely stay open. After tucking her in, I lie down next to her.

"You probably won't remember most of tonight when you wake up in the morning, but I'm going to say this because you should know. I haven't met anyone in a long time who I wish wasn't temporary."

She snuggles against me. "I like you."

I don't know if she even realizes she's petting my pecs again. "I like you, too."

"Would you ask me out on a date if I lived here?" Her words come out slow and soft.

"I'd do everything I could to make you fall in love with me if you were local."

Her hand stills. I think she's going to respond to my crazy declaration.

Instead, she presses a kiss on my chest. In seconds her breathing deepens and she falls asleep.

I promise myself I'll get up in a minute.

Or two.

I wake with a start. I fell asleep in my clothes.

It's still dark out, which means I'm not late for work, but I have no idea what time it is.

Mara is lying curled around me, one leg thrown over my thigh and her hands resting on my chest.

I smile at the memory of her touching me last night. My morning wood presses against my jeans—a painful reminder nothing happened.

If I didn't have to be on the mountain this morning, I'd wait for her to wake up and make love to her.

Slipping out of bed, I stand and scan the room for my phone.

I have an hour to get home and get to work. There's no time to do anything but say good-bye.

I kiss the top of her head and tuck the comforter around her. She snuggles deeper into the pillows.

In the living room I discover a notepad and leave a quick note.

For the first time in months, I'm awake with a smile on my face. The heaviness and anger living in my chest are gone.

Out on the sidewalk, I find her window and pause.

I could call in sick. Go back inside and wake her up.

I know I won't do either of those things, but for a brief moment, I want to.

TWENTY-FIVE

MARA

"GET DRESSED. I want you to show you something." He kisses my neck as I wash our breakfast dishes.

The scent of bacon and maple syrup still hangs in the air. I inhale deeply. He's bare chested because I'm wearing his shirt. Stealing his shirt is a two-fer: I love being wrapped in his scent, and Jesse in only jeans might be my new favorite thing. We've spent the morning hanging out in my apartment and it's been blissfully normal.

"Like if you show me yours, I have to show you mine? Haven't we been doing that. Twice last night and once this morning in the shower."

His warm lips skim my jaw. "No, something . . . serious."

I stop laughing and face him. "How serious? Like a STD serious?"

"I thought we've established I'm more of a hermit than a whore." His warm caramel eyes hold nothing but sincere truth.

"True that." I give him a soft kiss.

"Trust me?" He sounds a little nervous.

"I do." I don't pause to think about it.

I reluctantly peel off his shirt and get dressed in my own

boring clothes that don't smell like him.

Our fingers remain intertwined as we descend the stairs and walk outside. With a tug, he pulls me in the direction of his SUV parked next to my car. I follow without protest because I do trust him.

We drive toward Aspen. At the roundabout, he turns right, taking us down a road I've never seen before. We're still technically in Aspen, but the neighborhood is unfamiliar to me.

I'm about to ask if he's showing me where he buries the bodies when he pulls down a narrow, unpaved drive.

At the cemetery.

"Don't freak out." He's watching me like he expects me to panic.

"I'm not." I totally am. "This is . . . different."

"I want to explain where my head was at when we first met two years ago."

Nervous for a serious conversation, I run my finger along the stitching next to my thigh on the seat. "You don't owe me any explanations, not now, and not then. We were strangers."

"We're not anymore. It's important." I lift my eyes at the tone in his voice. The energy in the car has shifted from our usual joking self-protection to something real. It's terrifying.

"Okay." I nod.

He waits for me in front of the hood. When I reach him, he takes my hand and laces our fingers together.

"I don't handle death well. I hate animal movies because there's always death in them. I avoid funerals and usually hold my breath when I pass a cemetery." I blurt all of this in a continuous stream without breathing.

"Don't hold your breath now. I'm here. It's all good." He gives me a soft, half-smile and squeezes my hand.

"Weirdest date ever," I whisper as I drag my feet behind him. This is going to be serious. I don't always handle big issues well. I deflect with humor and avoidance.

Jesse leads me to a row of graves along a bluff. Below us the Roaring Fork river cuts its way through town. Multi-million dollar homes look down from Red Mountain. "It's a beautiful view."

Which none of the residents of the cemetery can enjoy.

"It is. It's a nice place to spend time." His voice is soft and he gives my hand a squeeze.

"Or all of eternity." I slap my hand over my mouth. "I'm sorry. I'm an asshole."

He chuckles. "Cody would've loved your lack of filter."

It finally hits me why we're here. His brother is buried along this ridge. I spot his headstone among the others. A simple gray slab of granite carved with mountains. My nerves buzz like an angry hive of bees. Jesse stops in front of his brother's grave and wraps his arm around me.

"Cody, this is Mara," he says softly.

I wave.

Jesse laughs.

"Oh right, he can't see me." I cover my face. "Hi."

"He can't hear you either."

I don't know what to do with myself. I've never met a dead person before.

This moment is important and I'm ruining it with being awkward. I focus on the epitaph carved into the granite. "I am free."

"It's a line from a John Denver song," Jesse explains.

I nod and read the rest of the engraving, "Cody Cerro Hayes, May 27, 1991—January 1, 2015. Beloved son, brother, friend."

"I wanted to add 'selfish-asshole' at the end, but was vetoed by the rest of the family. Cody would've agreed with me. I know it would make him laugh."

"You're so calm about this." I lean against his side.

He lets go of my hand and pulls me close. "I've had a couple of years to adjust. When you leapt into my arms at the Onion, everything was still raw. I was pissed off, hurt, and numb. Going through the motions of living, not really awake."

"Understandable . . . How did he die?" I know I can find out online, but I want Jesse's version, not a twisted tabloid story.

"Bike crash." The words lack emotion.

"Like a motorcycle?"

"No, he was on a mountain bike."

Makes sense given he was an adrenaline junkie. "Sounds like he died doing what he loved."

Jesse shakes his head. "He was drunk and riding the wrong way through traffic at the beach in San Diego. Car pulled out and hit him."

I don't know what to say, so I remain quiet.

He squeezes my arm. "He wasn't wearing a helmet because he thought he was invincible."

Suddenly his gift of a ski helmet doesn't feel so random.

"When I got the call, I thought his friends were joking. I hung up on them. There was no way my brother could be dead. He was one of those people who sucked every drop out of life, living high off of adrenaline and adventure. No way would he die riding a bike down a street. Too basic. If he was going to die, he'd go out spectacularly, pushing himself to a new record or a jump no one else has ever managed. God, I was pissed at him for being reckless and stupid."

Wrapping my arms around his waist in a side hug, I listen as he vents.

If his dog or cat died, I'd know what to say. I'd talk about the temporality of life and how lucky we are to love and be loved. Depending on how sentimental he is, I might offer a copy of the Rainbow Bridge poem. People are different. We have layers upon layers of emotional ties to the people in our lives, be they family or friends. No matter the status of those relationships at the time of the death, loss is loss, and it's never easy to say good-bye.

I don't realize I'm crying until the tears slide down my cheeks.

"Please don't be sad." Jesse kisses the top of my head.

I shrug and sniffle.

"Please don't. Cody hated sadness. Said life was too short to spend it miserable." He releases a small sigh.

"Well, he's not here to see it." I wipe my damp face.

"Fine. I hate it when people cry and I can't do anything to fix it."

"Sometimes people are sad. Like when they're standing next to a grave of someone who died way too young."

Jesse winds his other arm around my shoulders. "I'm sorry."

"For what?"

"Bringing you here."

I blow out a long, shaky breath. "I'm not. Cody's important to you."

He turns me in his arms so we're facing again. "I brought you here, because you're important to me. I want you to know me. All of me. My history, my dreams."

Is it wrong to make out in a graveyard? Will the dead care? Because his words make me want to do naughty things to him.

While I'm debating my next move, he kisses me. There's zero hesitation or second-guessing. His mouth softly presses against mine, and before I can overthink it, I'm kissing him back.

His arm tightens around me while his other hand cups my cheek. I press myself closer and weave my hands around his waist. Cursing the layers of coats and clothes between us, I still manage to squeeze his ass. It should be memorialized in marble.

Our kiss shifts into soft, gentle brushes of lips against one another before he breaks away. My breath comes in pants as

I try to recover.

Someone coughs nearby.

My eyes bug open and I try to jump away from him, but I'm still caged within his arms. So instead of a clean getaway, I squirm and twist like a fish on a line.

Jesse laughs at my flailing. "We're not doing anything wrong."

"Do you make out in churches, too?"

He laughs, and then releases me, but grabs my hand.

The only other person crazy enough to be in a snow-covered graveyard in March is a short man in an old-fashioned overcoat, wearing a cap last seen in a production of *Newsies*.

"Don't let me interrupt." He grins at us from a few feet away. In his hand he holds a bouquet of plastic flowers. "I'm glad to see young love is alive and well."

"We're not—" I begin to say, but Jesse interrupts me.

"You weren't."

He waves us off. "I used to sneak into the local cemetery with girls when I was a teenager. Almost zero chance of being discovered, especially if you go at night. Most folks would never think to go to one after dark. Spooked by the idea of ghosts. But if you think about it, you won't find a more private place to be alone."

The little old man is a class A Romeo. I bet he had all sorts of women on the line when he was younger. I stare at his face under his old-fashioned cap and try to imagine the man he used to be. It's not difficult to see the twinkle in his eye.

"We didn't come here to make out—"

"Excellent advice—"

Jesse and I speak at the time. I give him major side-eye.

As we stand together, our new friend pulls a mini of Bailey's out of his pocket. "Amelia loved her afternoon cocktail."

He opens the bottle, sips about half of it down, and then

pours the rest onto the snow near the flower carved headstone. After he sets the roses on the headstone, he kisses his fingers. "Happy Birthday, sweetheart."

We stand quietly for a moment in respect.

He clears his throat again before speaking. "Life's never long enough if you love someone." He tips his cap and walks toward the main entrance.

Jesse and I remain standing in silence for a minute or two.

Finally, I speak. "If I turn around and there are no footsteps in the snow, I'm really going to lose my mind."

His shoulders vibrate with laughter. "You think he was a ghost?"

Closing my eyes, I turn around. "Are there roses on the grave?"

"No." He almost pulls off sounding serious.

"No Bailey's flavored snow?"

"Who would waste perfectly good Bailey's by pouring it on the snow?"

I peel open one eye and confirm the footsteps in the snow and the roses on the grave. "If this were a movie, he'd be the ghost of love past."

"This is real life. There are no such things as ghosts. When we're gone, we're gone. Ashes to ashes."

Says the guy bringing a woman to his brother's grave.

"Before you can call me a hypocrite, I know Cody's not in there." He nods toward the headstone. "I don't know why I brought you here. I could've told you all of this in a warm bar where drinks are poured in glasses and not on the ground."

I step up on my toes to kiss his cold cheek. "Thank you."

"Ready to go?" He drapes an arm around my shoulders.

I nod and wave at his brother's grave. "Bye, Cody. You're brother's pretty amazing."

"He can't hear you."

"I know. I said it more for you."

Leaning down, he gives me a quick peck on my lips. "Thank you."

TWENTY-SIX

JESSE

A WEEK AFTER my weird trip with Mara to the cemetery, Abe and I are on avalanche patrol. We take the snowmobile to the boundary of the ski area to check out a reported avalanche after we got dumped with a foot of snow overnight. Abe carries the explosive kit in case we need to blast potentially dangerous build-up on the trails.

When I said Cody wasn't in there, I meant it. For my grandmother's sake, we interred some of his ashes in the cemetery. Old school and superstitious, she prepaid for the headstones and bought the row of plots next to my grandfather. A year after Cody died, we buried her next to her husband. I guess I should've introduced Mara to the rest of the Hayes clan buried alongside Cody, but meeting one dead family member was enough for one day.

"Looks like there was a natural slide in the out of bounds area last night or earlier this morning. I don't see any tracks." Abe points to the small debris field on the other side of the rope separating the ski area from out of bounds. The snow looks like someone stirred it with a big fork.

"Think we'll need to blast again?" I ask. Abe's the resident explosives guy, aka the coolest guy on patrol.

"Depends on how much snow we get tonight. All this heavy spring snow on top of the crappy base could slide down the slope like it's on ball bearings."

"Like resting blocks on sugar granules." I poke the snow with my ski pole. "Let's hope there's enough solid pack underneath. Ready?"

"Hopefully we're lucky and the slide took care of the tension." He pulls down his goggles. "Let's do this."

I hop over the crest and ski down the run, making wide, sweeping curves to check out the conditions. Fresh powder covers my legs up to the knees. My boots and skis disappear in the white, creating a wake of spray behind me.

I live for mornings like this. Being the first person to ski a run is heaven.

A few minutes later I hear and feel a loud *whompf* sound and check over my shoulder. Abe's about thirty yards above me, having taken his first turn on the steepest section of the slope.

Between us is a slide heading straight for me.

"Slide," I yell as loud as I can and wave him away. He pulls back and heads to the other side, the part of the slope not moving.

I have two choices: try to outrun the avalanche or ski out of its way. I have about two second to make any sort of escape. "Shit."

There's no way I can out-pace the wall of snow, so I head toward the tree line.

Stupid mistake.

I'm skiing on a moving wave of snow and not gaining any ground. More and more snow builds up around me and I know I'm caught.

Grabbing at the strap across my chest, I make sure my beacon is activated before pressing talk on my radio

"Ski patrol." Steve's on dispatch.

"Avalanche."

I get the words out as I'm pushed forward and begin to tumble. I pull the cord and an inflatable ring expands around my head, protecting my head and creating a pocket of air for me. Fatalities in avalanches are mostly from suffocation.

I know I'm still going downhill, but snow surrounds me. I have no idea if I'm covered by a few inches or a few feet. The sound of snow rumbling deafens everything.

Thank God I'm wearing my helmet and goggles. My pack and parka provide some additional padding as I'm shoved around by shifting blocks of snow as heavy as cement.

The sky breaks into my view for a few seconds. I gulp a mouth of fresh air and pray I'm okay.

Snow continues to roar and slide around me, churning me back under before I can get my bearings. I'm pretty sure I've lost a ski and both of my poles, but I can't see my hands.

My only reality right now is roiling snow and praying I don't get slammed into a tree or break my neck.

Dying in an avalanche is not how I'm going out. I know the stats. If Abe isn't caught, he'll have already radioed our location. The avalanche team will be on their way.

What feels like falling forever finally stops. Abruptly as it started, it's over. I open my eyes, hoping for ski and trees, but I'm surrounded by muted blue light.

I'm alive.

For now.

I do a quick mental assessment of my body. Nothing is screaming like it's broken. I wiggle my fingers. I can feel them. That's good. Same with my toes. Excellent. No spinal injury.

Not sure which way is up, I study the color of the snow. The lighter the blue, the closer I am to the surface. Complete blackness would be the worst-case scenario here.

Houston, we have blue snow!

Which is always better than yellow or brown snow.

While I'm able to wiggle my fingers, I can't move my arms. One is pinned across my chest. The other is pressed against my side. Or at least I think it is.

Fern will find me.

Shit. No, she won't. She's at the ranch with Mara.

I trust Abe and Zane one hundred percent. I know they're the best team on the mountain. But it's not the same.

Having faith I'll be freed soon, I focus on keeping my breathing steady so I don't hyperventilate or pass out. Mara's going to freak out when she discovers I've been in an avalanche. She's still skittish about the mountains. Unlike my brothers and me, she didn't grow up living and breathing the adrenaline only life in the mountains can provide. I'm not a risk junkie like Cody. Nor am I a boring office dweller like Wyatt, who lives in Denver with only a distant view of the mountains. I've tried to contain my wild side through ski patrol. Facing the reality of risks gone wrong helps ground me. Unlike Cody, I'm okay living with limits. I like being boring and I'm okay with being alone.

Or I was.

Mara has changed that.

Life isn't about cheating death or hiding from it.

We're here to enjoy being alive and if we're lucky, sharing our life with someone else.

Mara is my someone.

The snow above me crunches and shifts. Barking and voices filter through the dense pack.

Black paws break through the blue snow. Sunlight filters through the whiteness until I see blue sky.

"We thought we lost you." Abe's face appears above the hole. I've never been happier to see his scraggly beard.

"It's good to be found." I smile up at him.

TWENTY-SEVEN

MARA

JESSE ALMOST DIED yesterday.

He keeps telling me he didn't.

I remind him he had a near death experience.

He assures me he's fine.

Avalanches are great white walls of death.

He says they happen all the time.

He could've been killed.

He reminds me he's the one who called to tell me about the slide.

At first he left out the part about being buried alive.

He thought I'd freak out.

How silly.

To celebrate not being dead, he's taking me to dinner.

By dog sled. He called Mr. Anderson and asked for a favor. Our driver, Rogan, stands at the back of the wooden sled, steering the team of ten happy, barking malamutes along a groomed trail through bare aspen trees and tall pines. The twilight sky casts everything in a blue light and the snow glimmers purple against the growing shadows. Jesse and I sit under a pile of cozy blankets in the chilly night air.

"This is the single most romantic thing to ever happen to me. Or anyone. I'm willing to throw down with anyone who challenges me."

"Throw down? Really? Have you ever thrown down with anyone before? What do you even mean?" He bites the inside of his cheek to avoid laughing at me.

"I'm a scrapper. I have secret ninja skills." I make a karate chop in his general direction, which isn't easy to do given we're wrapped in blankets on a sled speeding through the winter twilight. I overestimate my chop and end up bonking him in the nose.

"Ouch!" His hands come up to cover his face, muffling his voice. "Okayibelifyou."

"I'm so sorry. I've ruined our romantic moment."

I notice his shoulders are shaking. It could be the motion of the sled as we fly over the snow behind a team of dogs. Or he's crying from pain.

"Are you okay?" I've broken his nose. Worst thing ever.

I can hear the sound of his sobbing. I've brought the man to tears.

Hold on, that's not the sound of crying. He's laughing.

"You're faking!" I twist away from him, but there's really nowhere for me to go given I'm sitting in his lap.

His eyes become visible as he spreads his fingers over his face. "Is it safe or are you planning to go all ninja on me again?"

"You're officially shunned." I cross my arms to emphasize I'm done.

"I've never been assaulted by someone wearing mittens before." He wraps his arms around me in a hug . . . or to restrain me.

"This might not be the last time with your attitude." I stick my tongue out.

"No more mittens for you. You're reverting to being eight

and throwing snowballs at me."

I make a sour face. "Ugh. You don't want to know the eight-year-old me. Total nerd with frizzy hair and an overbite."

He leans down, closer to my ear. I feel his warm breath on my skin when he speaks, low and growly. "Go on . . . I've always had a thing for smart women. My first crush was the school librarian."

He runs his hand down the side of my neck before tilting me back to him.

I inhale as he presses his mouth against mine. The heat of his mouth contrasts against the cold air, warming my lips with his own. Still attached to me at the mouth, he leans us forward to reclaim the blanket, cocooning us underneath the thick wool.

Beneath the added privacy, his hand leaves my neck and skims over my shoulder before finding my breast. I'm wearing too many layers, but somehow the heat and pressure from his palm penetrates down to my bare skin. I shiver, but not from the cold.

I want, no I need, more of his touch. Feeling bold, I guide his hand between my bent legs and press. "There."

"We have an audience," he whispers against my mouth.

"He can't see anything. We're buried under blankets." I suck his tongue into my mouth, brushing it with my own. Pretending the world doesn't exist outside of the two of us sounds perfect to me.

"He can still hear us," Jesse whispers against my lips. He presses his hard length against my butt. I'm not the only one affected by our impromptu make-out session.

"Shh, the dogs will hear you and get spooked." I wiggle in his lap, not-so-secretly loving to torture him.

His laughter brushes against my cheek. "Can you promise to be quiet yourself?"

Biting the finger of one of his gloves, he slowly drags it off.

It's a hand striptease and oddly sexy. He sweeps his palm south over my breasts and waist. When I feel his warm fingers flex along my inner thigh, I nod and manage to squeak out a "yes."

"Shh." He quiets my sounds with a searing kiss when he dips his hand beneath my leggings.

He skims his fingers inside my underwear and I say a small thanks to whoever invented Lycra as well as the brave women who fought against the stigma of leggings as pants. *Bless you all.*

A string of vowel sounds fall from my lips, because all I can do is whimper with joy.

Jesse is a giver.

Oh, and before I get completely distracted, thanks to whoever invented blankets.

His magic fingers explore and torture me while we glide over hill and vale in our own personal winter wonderland. I'm not paying attention to any of the scenery. Not anymore. I close my eyes to focus on the sensation building where his hand touches me. Every nerve ending fires as he presses his thumb against my clitoris while stroking two fingers inside of me.

Pleasure and pressure combine together, lifting me to a breaking point. I need to bite down or I'll scream out his name. Breaking our kiss, I find the skin where his shoulder meets neck and silence my cries with a bite, riding out the waves of pleasure pulsing through my body.

I still his hand as the last flutters of my orgasm fade.

"Did you draw blood?" he whispers as he slides his fingers out of my pants.

I soothe the patch of skin with my tongue. "No, but I can't promise you won't have a hickey there later."

Embarrassed, I can barely lift my eyes to his. "Sorry about the biting. I didn't want to scare the dogs by screaming your name and having it echo over the mountains. The hills are alive with Mara's orgasm and all that jazz."

He chuckles and then does the sexiest thing. Keeping his gaze locked with mine, he sucks his fingers into his mouth and hums with satisfaction.

"Kill me now," I whisper, mainly to myself.

"What was that?" His voice has an edge of danger and lust. Like he's taking my words as a challenge to orgasm me to death.

"Nothing."

He leans close again, taking my bottom lip between his and gently nipping the swollen skin. "I can't wait to taste you for real later."

Incoherent vowel sounds catch in my throat.

Our sled glides to a stop and I panic. Pulling the blanket completely over our heads, I hide my face in Jesse's shoulder.

"Is he kicking us out of the sleigh for indecency?"

Jesse shakes his head. "No, I think we've arrived at the lodge."

I drop one corner of the blanket to check our surroundings. Twinkling stars, silver snow-covered trees, and the warm exhales of the dogs are the first things I notice. Turning my head to Jesse's side of the sleigh, I realize we're parked outside a charming cabin straight out of Heidi. Torches and tiny lights brighten the exterior.

The inside of the lodge, I fully expect Swiss milkmaids to yodel while men in Lederhosen dance around in clogs. Instead, he leads me to a table by an enormous stone fireplace. Candles in glass jars of all shapes and sizes illuminate the room. Because of the soft light inside, the snowy landscape glows on the other side of the window. A million plus stars sparkle above the sharp peaks. We're inside our own winter wonderland.

I glance around and realize we're the only people in the restaurant.

"Where is everyone?"

"They're not usually open on Mondays." He shrugs like it's no big deal.

"Another favor?" I twist my fingers between his on the table.

"I came to some realizations today."

"While you were buried alive?" My eyes tingle as they fill with tears.

"Shh. Stop. I'm fine." He soothes me with a soft voice.

My lip trembles and I fail to smile.

"Mara, I'm okay. I'm here with you because today I realized there's nowhere I'd rather be."

Cue full waterworks. "With me?"

"With you." He lifts our joined hands. "I love you."

I want to tell him it's too soon. He doesn't really mean it. I should warn him I'm crazy and want to be a cat lady. He should wait until he knows me better. For once, I don't say any of the craziness in my head. "I love you."

The dimple of suppressed amusement appears. His eyes smile before his mouth follows in a glorious, beautiful grin.

"I'm crazy," I tell him. "You should be warned."

He leans across the table and kisses me. "It's okay, because I'm crazy over you."

TWENTY-EIGHT

MARA

DISAPPEARING SNOW AND longer days mark the middle of April. With the change in season comes another round of crazy local traditions.

Schneetag is the end of season party in Snowmass. It's basically a free-for-all day of silliness involving costumes, a large pond of icy water, homemade contraptions, and a per capita alcohol consumption to rival Mardi Gras in New Orleans.

Or so I've been told.

Legend has it all the rugby guys wear dresses as part of their costumes. Now that's something I need to see.

Sofie's here visiting and I'm happy how well she fits in with my new friends.

Sage, Zoe, Mae, and the rest of the girl gang meet at the shuttle stop at the end of Brush Creek in Snowmass. Apparently, making someone be the designated driver was deemed cruel and unusual punishment.

The shuttle's packed with the oddest assortment of people, including not one, but three unicorns.

Our rainbow of wigs and wings seems tame compared to most of the costumes.

Zoe and Sage talk about Lee's red sparkly dress from last year.

"Easley didn't even shave his back. He looked like a two-hundred-pound gorilla going to prom," Mae giggles.

"When doesn't he look like a gorilla?" Sage snorts.

Picking on Easley seems to be the common thread of most of their conversations. Seems he's an easy target. He's always been nice to me. No one mentions Landon given we all agree he's a giant tool.

Jesse's name doesn't come up and I begin to wonder if he participates in the silliness. He's such a recluse, I can't really see him being silly enough to ski into a pond in front of a huge crowd.

"What about ski patrol? Do they participate?"

Sage and Zoe make eye contact before Sage faces me. "They're the finale every year. Prepare yourself."

Zoe giggles. "One year Speedos were involved and there were several wardrobe malfunctions."

Mae leans over and whisper shouts near my ear, "Penises for days. Turns out shrinkage is a real affliction. It looked like a turtle parade when they crawled out of the water."

The rest of the girls cackle.

"You've never laughed so hard in your life." Mae winks at me. "We say a little prayer of a repeat every year."

With the lifts closing and the ski season officially ending, everything feels like the end of summer camp. Some of us are full time, year rounders, but a lot of people will move on to their next gig. A few of the hardcore ski instructors and patrol head south, way south, to South America to follow the snow. Anyone with a seasonal contract takes off until the weather cools in the fall. They return with the first talk of snow. Like flocks of birds, except they follow the cold weather.

I'm looking forward to seeing what the mountains are like

in the summer and fall. At least Sage, Zoe, and Mae will all stick around.

Jesse owns his place and works construction when there isn't snow on the ground. I assume this means he isn't going anywhere, but we haven't had the big talk about future plans. Or even what we're doing this summer. We've only known each other four months, but it feels longer.

I remind myself he's in love with me. That's everything I need to know to be happy in this moment. I'm not going to worry about what comes next. This winter I've learned you have to take life as it comes. I can handle anything, one mogul at a time.

Fern's healed nicely from her cut, but she still spends time at the ranch with Tapper and the cats. I think she and Tapper are having a mad love affair. Jesse doubts me, but who's the professional here? Even the cats have welcomed her into the family . . . by being assholes. It's how they show their love.

The shuttle arrives at base village and we join the massive crowd of other crazy people in costumes walking toward the slopes.

Excitement fills the air. Loud dance music pumps through huge speakers near the DJ booth. Women in bikinis and fur boots laugh until they fall into a bank of snow. Men cheer each other on in a game of beer pong. The whole scene reminds me of the love child between a rave and spring break.

"Rainbow Bright, I love you!" Some random guy in a tutu grabs Sofie and kisses her.

"I love you too!" she shouts after he stumbles away.

"Do you know him?" I ask.

"Never seen him before and probably will never see him again. Or maybe I will." She grins. "Welcome to Schneetag!"

We dance our way through the crowd to the edge of the pond and claim a spot in front of the barricade.

The DJ lowers the music and announces the first teams are in position to start the main show. Everyone goes wild when two guys in huge wigs and flight attendant costumes slide down the ramp in a tiny airplane. They topple over before reaching the water, but no one seems to care.

More crazy costumes follow. Stormtroopers roll a giant Death Star into the pond and then jump in behind it. A group of bikini-clad girls in giant, furry cat heads follow them, but chicken out before going into the water. More than a few on-lookers boo.

Only one man in a cardboard box on skis makes it across the pond without sinking. The judges give him all nines and tens as we all wildly cheer for his engineering mastery.

Sage whoops extra loud as the next group takes their place at the top of the slope. "It's the rugby club!"

I squint into the bright April sun. "Are you sure?"

"Oh yes, I recognize Lee's silver dress."

"Silver dress?" I repeat unnecessarily as the group of burly players wearing tiny silver dresses and shiny helmets pushes a spacecraft down the hill.

"They're going too fast," Zoe shouts next to me.

Sure enough the spacecraft shoots out of Lee's grip and Easley falls on his face trying to slow it down. The cardboard disk gains impressive air and flies into the middle of the pond, where it immediately sinks.

Only one judge holds up her card displaying a ten while the rest give the guys sevens and eights.

Lee drags himself out of the water and finds Sage in the crowd. He gives her a giant wet hug and a sloppy kiss while she squirms in his arms, trying to stay dry.

Spying me over his shoulder, he grins. "Hi, Mara. Wait until you see Jesse."

The DJ gets everyone riled up with his chanting for ski

patrol. The frenzy grows when he switches songs. Drumming echoes through the air. "Are you ready?"

We shout and scream, "Yes!"

"I can't hear you." He stops the music. "I said, are you ready?"

Zoe, Sofie, and Mae scream in both my ears to the point I hear ringing.

"Making the final run of the season, here are the men and women of ski patrol. Give it up and show them the love!"

People lose their minds when the first notes of music play.

My eyes are glued to the top of the slope, waiting for Jesse.

I don't even realize what music is playing until Abe and Johan walk out wearing red one-piece bathing suits.

Women's bathing suits.

I think I stop breathing as everyone jumps and claps around me.

Jesse joins the group, wearing a red ski jacket and shorts. In his hands he's holding what looks like a giant red plastic football.

"Oh my dog." No one can hear me over the *Baywatch* theme song and screaming.

He spins the red tube and then tosses it to Abe.

Turning around, he slowly peels off his ski jacket and wiggles out of his shorts.

Leaving him standing up there in nothing but a red Speedo.

Every ovary in the crowd simultaneously explodes.

"That's your man," Sofie whisper-shouts near my ear. "You lucky girl."

I try to close my mouth, but it hangs open in shock.

The ski patrollers run down the hill in slow motion. At least it feels that way while I stare at Jesse.

When they reach the bottom, they jump into the pool in unison.

Mayhem breaks out as others join them, not caring about

the cold water or hypothermia.

I can't see Jesse in all the chaos, so I duck under the barrier and run to the edge.

He's a few feet away, grinning up at me.

I leap, knowing he'll catch me.

EPILOGUE

JESSE

THE FIRST REAL snow of the season dumped a foot of glorious powder on the mountain last week. Seven months of no skiing makes me a little crazy. I'm happiest when I'm on the mountain with my girls.

Fern is back to her normal self and I can tell she's as ready to get back to work as I am. She's spent the summer lazing around the ranch with Tapper. Mara even bought a kiddie pool for them. We're all spoiled by her love. Especially me.

The lifts officially opened yesterday and this is the first time we've skied together since April. A pale November sun glowing in the clear sky promises a great day of skiing.

Mara eyes the sign for Powderhorn. "You want to revisit the scene of the crime?"

"Our meeting was a crime?" I pull one of her curls sticking out below her helmet.

"Second meeting." She grins at me.

"I want to show you something."

She narrows her eyes at me. "Last time you said that, we made out with dead people."

I fight the urge to laugh. She's as funny as she is beautiful.

Her forehead crinkles. "Wait, that didn't come out right. You know what I mean. You were there with me."

I chuckle. "I remember."

"Can the thing you show me not involve a panic attack or death?" Even as she says this, she's pulling on her goggles and adjusting her gloves.

"I'll make sure you get down safely. Trust me?"

"With my life. Apparently," she mumbles against my mouth as I try to kiss her.

We successfully ski down the first section of Powderhorn. After a couple of lessons last season, she's built up her confidence enough she doesn't hesitate to follow in my tracks. Sometimes she races beside me if she's feeling extra bold. When we hit the stretch of the run that doubles as a fire road in the dry season, I slow enough for her to ski alongside me. To the left, a steep drop-off opens up the view to the back of Mount Daly across a narrow valley. Our destination is up ahead. Before she goes flying by it, I reach out my hand, hoping she understands I want to hold hands. She gets the message and grabs on to my glove.

Instead of making the turn to finish the run, I slow to a stop by the bench.

Snow covers the area around it but the sun has warmed the bench, leaving it bare.

"Let's sit." I gesture with my pole.

"Here?"

"It's a bench. It exists to be sat upon." I pull her closer and she lets herself slide forward.

"Poor, lonely bench. Why are you in the middle of nowhere? You'd be a lot more popular in a park." She pats the seat before sitting down.

I hold my breath, but she doesn't notice the plaque on the back.

"Wow. It's beautiful." She sweeps her gaze over the valley below us.

"I agree." I've seen this view hundreds of time. I'm talking about her.

She faces me. "You're not even looking at the incredible beauty of nature on display right over there."

She points somewhere over to her right.

"I have all the natural beauty right in front of me."

Her eyes narrow. "You're putting on the charms a little thick today. The time for pickup lines has passed, don't you think? I'm already madly in love with you."

"Are you saying my best moves are cheesy? I'm wounded." I press my glove against my chest.

"You don't need to pick me up. Unless you're physically carrying me to bed." She licks her lips and winks.

"You're adorable."

"I'm trying to seduce you." She pouts.

"Consider yourself successful. I'm yours."

"We did this backward."

"In what sense?"

"We met, kissed, had imaginary terrible sex, and then got to know each other."

I start to correct her, but she stops me.

"I spent two years thinking we had bad sex."

"Those are years you'll never get back. You lost all that time."

"Better than pining for someone I could never have."

I kind of like the idea of her pining. "You weren't the only one who pined. I'm the one who remembered every detail. For two years, I lived with the memory of your kiss, thinking I'd missed my chance with you."

She kisses my cheek. "If you remember everything, can you answer a question for me?"

"I'll try."

"What was up with the kazoo?"

My laugh peals through the silence around us. "I forgot about that. Someone handed it to you as we left Escobar's."

"Did I play it?" She covers her face with her gloved hand

I lower her fingers so I can see her eyes. "Let's say you shouldn't quit your day job to join a kazoo band."

Mara closes her eyes and shakes her head. "I'm a nut. Yet you still pined for me?"

I nod and kiss her softly on the mouth. "Obviously, I'm crazy, too."

She leans her head against my shoulder. "If we hooked up for real back then, it would've been a disaster. Long distance? Vet school? Terrible combination."

"Plus, I wasn't in the headspace for anything more."

"And now?" Her voice is hesitant.

I hate that.

"Remember our misguided visit to the cemetery?"

"I'll never forget."

"I've never brought a girl there. Or here."

She shifts to face me, giving me the encouragement to continue.

"Love doesn't dwell in the past. It lives in the present—in our hearts and the memories we carry with us. Love resides in sunshine and our laughter. Everywhere we look, in every beautiful view, we feel love."

Her eyes well up. "Did you just make that up?"

"I wish. Cody wrote it." I point to the brass plaque on the top slat of the bench.

"In memory of Cody Hayes. His spirit and love for the mountains lives on." Her voice cracks at the end of the sentence.

Lifting her chin, I press my lips on her wet cheek before staring into her beautiful eyes.

"You are my love."

This snow will melt, the hills will green and fade to brown, the aspen leaves will turn gold before the first snowflakes blanket the mountains with white again.

Our life together is only beginning. If we're lucky, we'll have decades to love each other. We're looking at property where I can build a house for us. Someday soon I'll bring her back here and propose, making her mine forever. A few years later, we'll ski these slopes with our own kids.

Between now and then, I'm going to love Mara every minute of every day we have together.

A NOTE FROM DAISY

THANK YOU FOR reading.

I hope you enjoyed *Crazy Over You*. This story was sparked during a visit to Snowmass Village, Colorado last September. When I saw a bench at the edge of a cliff, I knew I had to include it in a book. Yes, this is a love story inspired by a bench. If you're ever in Snowmass, hike the Ditch Trail or ski Powderhorn, and you'll find the real version of Cody's bench.

Love with Altitude is a new series for me. Book One, *Next to You*, is available on all ebook retailers. *Crazy Over You* is Book Two. Book Three, *Wild for You*, will be coming out later this year. Check out the first chapter of *Next to You* on the next page. Click to the end of this book for the buy-links for all of my current titles.

If you enjoyed Jesse and Mara's story, please consider donating to an animal shelter or rescue organization near you. My beloved ginger tabby, Pretty Boy Floyd, was a rescue cat who was returned twice before I adopted him. I'm not saying he was the inspiration for either Fred or George, but I'm not saying he wasn't.

I appreciate you taking the time to write an honest review and sharing it on Goodreads or your favorite retailer. Reviews and word of mouth are the best ways to spread the word about books we enjoy.

To keep up with my latest news and upcoming releases, sing up for my mailing list.

xo
Daisy

ABOUT DAISY

DAISY PRESCOTT IS the USA Today bestselling author of contemporary romantic comedies, including Modern Love Stories, the Wingmen series, and the Love with Altitude series.

Daisy currently lives in a real life Stars Hollow in the Boston suburbs with her husband, their rescue dog Mulder, and an indeterminate number of imaginary house goats. When not writing, she can be found in the garden or kitchen, lost in a good book, or on social media, usually talking about hot, bearded men and sloths.

www.daisyprescott.com

www.twitter.com/Daisy_Prescott

www.facebook.com/daisyprescottauthorpage

www.instagram.com/daisyprescott

ACKNOWLEDGMENTS

I'M THANKFUL MOST of all for my readers. Thank you for buying, reading, reviewing and sharing my books.

Big love and thanks to my husband for being my partner in all things. Many of the funny parts of this book are funnier because of your input and sense of humor. Thank you to my Colorado family for reminding me of the beauty of the Roaring Fork Valley and the joys of Ruggerfest last year. Our time together inspired this series.

To Julia Kent, thank you for being a beta reader, a sounding board, and a good friend. To the Indie community of smart, talented, driven, and generous authors, thank you for being amazing. I'm lucky to call you colleagues and friends.

MJ, thank you for reading an early version of this. It's better because of your input and cheerleading. I think I'll call you Maverick from now on.

To the members of Daisyland, thank you for being the best group of readers ever. I'm grateful every day for your friendship, your support, our conversations, and all of the sloths.

Special shout out to: Kiersten Hill at BFF Book Blog; Tina Lynne at Typical Distractions; Nic Farrell at Flirty and Dirty Book Blog; Laurie Oh and Nina Grinstead at The Literary Gossip; Amber Boyd at The Geekery Book Reviews; Mandy Lawler at Straight Shootin Book Reviews; Lori Wilt at Ficwishes; Dee Montoya at Wrapped up in Reading; Jennifer Beach at Uniquely Jenn; Autumn Davis at Agents of Romance; Debbie Besabella at Black Heart Reviews; Michelle Kannan at All Romance Reviews; Miranda at Red Cheeks Reads; Chanpreet Singh at Saucy Book Reviews; Phala at Aalya and Books; Erin Spencer at Southern Belle; Roxie Madar at Schmexy Girl; Vilma at Vilma's Book Blog; Melissa Krehley at Slow Reader's Blog; Lisa at True Story; Margie Longoria at Margie's Must Reads; Stacy Sanders at Red Reader's Reads; Tracey Kruger at Smut Book Junkie; and to every blogger who takes the time to write a read and write a review of one of my books, thank you! Your support is never taken for granted. Thank you for all that you do for the love of books.

Thank you for the beautiful cover and series branding, SM Lumetta. You are truly a magical unicorn. Christine, you make my words into gorgeous books and you're one of the nicest people in the world.

I'm blessed to have an amazing team of support: Fiona Fischer, my super kickass assistant; my expeditious editor Melissa Ringsted at There for You Editing; needle in the haystack finders, Marla Esposito of Proofing with Style and Elli Reid for proofreading; Jessica Estep at Inkslinger PR and Jeananna and Kylie at Give Me Books for helping to spread the word about my books; Meire Dias at Bookcase Literary Agency, who has become so much more than an agent; and KP Simmon at Inkslinger PR, for her wisdom and big picture vision. To each of you, a huge thank you for keeping me focused on my goals.

Most of all, thank you, readers, for leaving a review or telling a friend about my books.

Hearing from my readers is the best part of publishing. I can be reached on social media or at *daisyauthor@gmail.com*.

xo

Daisy